THE BOY
WHO HEARS
MUSIC

THE BOY
WHO HEARS
MUSIC

Robert Barlow Fox

SUNSTONE
PRESS

SANTA FE

Sunstone books may be purchased for educational, business, or sales promotional use. For information please write: Special Markets Department, Sunstone Press, P.O. Box 2321, Santa Fe, New Mexico 87504-2321.

Library of Congress Cataloging-in-Publication Data:
Fox, Robert B. (Robert Barlow), 1930–
   The boy who hears music / Robert Barlow Fox.
       p. cm.
ISBN: 0-86534-489-2 (pbk. : alk. paper)
1. Masai (African people)—Fiction. 2. Adopted children—Fiction.
3. Ranch life—Utah—Fiction. I. Title.

PS3556.O947B69 2006
813´.54—dc22

                                         2005057491

WWW.SUNSTONEPRESS.COM
SUNSTONE PRESS / POST OFFICE BOX 2321 / SANTA FE, NM 87504-2321 /USA
(505) 988-4418 / ORDERS ONLY (800) 243-5644 / FAX (505) 988-1025

PART I

LEAVING AFRICA

Each of us has our music
That is ours alone—
To dance to its rhythm
Or sing to its melody
And tap our feet
To its special beat...
Rarely just to listen.
Some hear their music loud and clear
As though it was very near.
Others just hear it as static
And too often not at all.
Hearing its special message
Is the important element...
Being properly tuned in.
We can all make the choice
Even if we hear our music
As just a still, small voice.
But we must learn to listen.
Listen!
Listen!

—R.B.F.

CHAPTER 1

It was to be his last trip abroad, a camera safari into Kenya and Tanzania, sponsored by the National Geographic Magazine, in return for an article and pictures. He would travel through the Serengeti Plains, the Great Rift Valley, Maasai Mara and many other game preserves.

This trip would have to be the last because arthritis and seventy-five years of earth life had brought a slump to his broad shoulders and a slight limp to his long legs. His frame, once tall and lean and straight as Abe Lincoln's, was showing the wear of time and travel, although enthusiasm within still moved his human machinery quite well.

Alfred King, lonely widower and multi-millionaire cattle rancher, was a member of the elite 100 Club, a rare conglomeration of international individuals who had traveled to at least 100 different countries. They were archaeologists, scientists, writers, geologists, anthropologists, teachers and adventurers who wanted to see the earth's geography, study its weather and climate and experience its many cultures. Alfred King wanted to meet its peoples... people were the important thing to him.

It was on the road to Amboselli, along the border between Tanzania and Kenya that he met the boy at a roadside rest stop. There was a wood and tin shack with an outdoor toilet in back. A table in front of the shack displayed carved objects for sale. A large metal tub was filled with bottles of soda pop. As soon as the old man got out of the van he was surrounded by native boys trying to sell him items. He shook his head and said, "No," several times before they gave up and wandered off. He slumped wearily to the ground in the sparse shade of the shanty, removed his wide brimmed safari hat and mopped his face with a handkerchief. The midday sun beat down relentlessly.

A small boy approached him hesitantly. "Mister, can I talk with you to practice my English?"

The old man looked up at the boy who was very black, which made his round eyes and smiling teeth look all the whiter. His head was shaved and a gold ring hung from each ear. He was naked except for dirty red boxer shorts. Alfred figured the boy to be maybe five, six or seven. Ages all seemed to slip by him now. He registered age in his mind as babies, kids, adults, and old age.

"Sure. Sit down here and let's talk. First, can I buy you a soda pop?"

"Yes. I would like that, Sir."

"Good. Get me one too," the old man said, handing the boy a five dollar bill. "What kinds do they have?"

"You have a choice of warm coca cola or warmer coca cola," replied the boy, showing his white teeth.

Alfred King chuckled. "I'll have a warm coca cola then."

The boy came back with two opened bottles of coke and gave the man one dollar change. "Two dollars a bottle is awful expensive coke," he remarked.

"Anything you get to drink out here is expensive," said the boy, sitting down facing the man. "Mostly because there just isn't much of anything to drink anywhere out here."

The old man tipped up the bottle and eagerly took several swallows. "What's your name, my friend?" he asked.

"It is too long for you to say. The Elders gave me a substitute name. I am called Koro. They told me it means old one. It is from a language that is not of my people. They gave me the name because they said that I think thoughts beyond my years... and that I follow my music." He looked shyly away.

"How many years are you?"

"Seven years. At least that is what I am told."

They both drank from the bottles. The old man wiped his face again with the handkerchief while the boy observed him. "You are very white," said the boy after awhile.

"Yes. That is true. I am what you would call a white man," he stammered, not knowing what else to say.

"I mean you are whiter than most white men. I have seen others. But you are whiter... your skin is pale. The hair of your beard and brows is as white as summer clouds, and your eyes the color of a clear sky."

The man was astounded and laughed hardily. "You are observant and speak like a poet. And you do think thoughts beyond your years. Your elders have named you well. Yes, I come from a pale line of people from the Scandinavian countries. Although I spend much of my time in the sun my skin doesn't burn or tan much." He studied this amazing small boy, who smiled openly at him. "I didn't notice any villages around here. Where do you come from?"

"By your way of measuring I live about twenty miles from here."

"Twenty miles! How do you get here?"

"I walk on my two strong feet and legs. If I am lucky, some times I catch a ride in a truck or on a bicycle."

"You walk? Twenty miles?"

"It is the only means of travel we have, Sir. All of our people walk except for a few wealthy ones who have acquired bicycles."

"And your parents let you come this far?" the old man asked, incredulously.

"I have no parents. I am accountable to the Elders of my tribe. My father was killed by a lion while tending our cattle many years ago. My mother ran away to the big city of Nairobi." He looked down at the ground. "I have a big brother, but he has turned very bad..."

"Bad in what way?"

"He has become a bandit. He has joined a robber band. They rob tourists along this very road. They come from the bushes over there in Tanzania to rob travelers here in Kenya and then they run back there to hide from the authorities. They might even rob you, Sir."

"My driver has a weapon."

"It would be useless against many robbers with many weapons."

"Yes, I have heard of such bandits."

They both finished their drinks in silence. After some time the man spoke again. "Since we are becoming friends, forgive me for not introducing myself. My name is Alfred King. But since I am to call you Koro, you will please call me Alf. And by the way, you don't need much practice speaking English. You speak better English than eighty percent of my people."

Koro smiled proudly at the compliment.

"How would you like to go to America with me, Koro?" The words just popped out of the old man's mouth. He didn't know how or why. He hadn't given it thought. The words almost spoke from their own power.

The boy looked stunned and couldn't speak for some time. "Do you mean that, Alf?

Do you mean that for real?"

"Yes. For real."

"I would like that very much. I would like to go to America with you more than anything in this world." Then he added apprehensively. "But this matter would have to be approved by the Elders of my clan."

"Here," Alfred King said, handing the boy money. "Buy us and our driver another warm coca cola and hop in the van. We are going to talk with your Elders."

CHAPTER 2

The van bounced and rumbled along the animal trail. They had left the main road, which hadn't been much better. The only way that the driver knew where to go was from Koro's directions. Dust arose and swirled around the vehicle like a brown mist. There was no breeze so the dust just settled back upon them. If they rolled up the windows of the van, the heat became unbearable.

None of these inconveniences seemed to affect Koro. "There are many tribes in our country," he was explaining. The driver remained silent, concentrating on the road, trying to avoid the worst pot holes. Alfred King had paid him extra for this side trip, and he was listening intently to this amazing boy.

"There are Bantu, Somburu, Kikuyu... but my tribe, the Maasai, is the most in number of all of the tribes," said Koro proudly.

"Are you happy in your country... with your people?" asked the pale skinned American.

"Oh yes. I am very happy. But, of course, I would be happy in America also. It is my desire to learn of other countries and other peoples. My music directs me toward this learning."

"You have spoken before of your music, Koro. I do not understand this. What is your music?"

The boy looked suddenly apprehensive and turned his gaze out of the window. He didn't speak again for a period of time. The old man wondered if he had offended him by asking such a personal question. He mopped his face again with the damp handkerchief. His shirt was also wet and clinging to his skin.

"Pass the water bag back, Anwar," he said to the driver, irritated with himself. He drank deeply. Koro shook his head when offered the water bag. The heat and dust did not seem to bother him.

After a long silence the boy spoke quietly. "I have decided to give you my complete trust, Alf, since I might be going to live with you. My music... it comes from out there somewhere... from another world. It is a music more beautiful than my words can explain. The music often directs me as to what I should do, how I should act, and what path to follow. Perhaps you will hear more about it from my people."

Then he abruptly changed the subject. "Now it is for you to tell me some things about yourself, Alf. What has brought you here to my country? You must be brave because you travel alone and not in a group as most tourists do."

"Brave? No. I am used to being by myself and adjust easily to strangers and situations."

"Do you not get lonely?"

"Not really. When I am lonely it doesn't last long. I like my own company and am at peace with myself, although I do enjoy being with others." He paused and a far away look clouded his eyes. "Like you, I have no family. My wife died many years ago, and my only son was killed in an airplane crash. I grieved for many years. Then suddenly I got on with the living of my life again. I became grateful for each new day and try to make the best of it. So, also like you, I am happy. I like to keep learning. There is so much to learn and we are here on this earth for such a short time."

"I think a lot like that, Alf. I think that we will be pleased with each other if I get to come with you."

"Yes, I believe that we will get along quite well," agreed the old man, smiling. "As to what I am doing in your country, I am taking pictures of the animals, the country and the people, and writing a story about it all for a magazine."

"One thing I must ask, Alf, is that when we are with my people that you do not take their pictures. Some of them would let you for money. Sadly they have learned of money. But it would offend some of the old ones. They still cling to the belief that if you take their picture you take away their spirits or even their souls. You can maybe get their pictures from far away if you have the camera I have heard of that does that."

"Yes. I have such a camera with a telephoto lens that brings far away objects up close. I am also aware of that belief of your people. I have traveled to many countries and I always honor the traditions and customs of the people."

"Have you always been a story writer and one who takes pictures?"

"It has been an interest and hobby of mine for many years. But I also have many other things that I do. My work or my job, which pays for my many hobbies, is cattle. I raise cattle."

The boy's eyes widened in excitement. "You have cattle? It is the main job of my people. Cattle are the life of my people."

Alfred King smiled warmly at his small friend. "I know that. It is another reason that we will get along well if you are allowed to come with me. My cattle are different than the cattle of your people. They are shorter and fatter. Their coloring is red and they have white faces. But you will like them. I have cowboys that work for me. They take care of them while I am away and also when I am home. There are four of them that are like my own sons. And one old man who does our cooking."

"Straight ahead, Anwar," the boy instructed the driver. "About three kilometers. You can see my village way up ahead."

CHAPTER 3

The van came to a stop and was swallowed in a cloud of brown dust. Three figures came out of the cloud coughing, sneezing and fanning the dust, which finally settled.

"This is my village," said Koro. "It is called in our language a *kraal* or *engang*. The thorny bushes which circle it are piled high to keep out wild animals. Come, Anwar. Come, Alf. Enter here through the gate and meet my people."

Inside the *kraal*, small huts formed a circle around the outside of the village. They looked like bowls turned upside down. In the center of the village children chased each other, playing games and laughing happily. Women and girls were making colorful beaded necklaces and other craft items. Older women were cooking over open fires. Men were sharpening knives and performing other chores. The men who had greeted them brought a tall, lean man to them. He was built and dressed like most of the men, but had an aura of authority about him. He wore a bright red toga or poncho over his shoulders that reached to his thighs. Beaded earrings dangled from each ear. He carried a spear-like staff about seven feet long.

"Welcome to our village," he said in perfect English, as he patted Koro affectionately on his bald head. "You may call me Ole."

"Ole, these are my friends," said Koro. "This is Alfred King from America, and this is Anwar, the vehicle driver."

"Friends of Koro are friends of our entire village," said Ole, smiling. "He is our most favored *Inkera* or youth. We have given him the title of *Laibon*, which means one with special powers. If he were even but a few years older he would be a spiritual leader, very rare for one so young, a title usually given to the very old. He has the special gift to hear music no one else can hear. It guides his path daily."

"May I ask, Ole, where you learned to speak English so eloquently?" asked Alfred King.

"I received some learning in your country, Mr. King, and some in the country of Great Britain. In fact I have received three of what you call diplomas or degrees from universities. I also speak several other languages."

"He is my teacher of your language," interrupted Koro proudly.

Ole smiled down at the boy. It was obvious how proud he was of the old fellow. "And now, Mr. King, may I ask what brings you to our country, and more specifically to our village."

"In answer to your first question, I came to your country to take pictures and write an article for National Geographic magazine. You might have heard of it."

"Indeed I have," said Ole. "And an interesting coincidence because I once contributed to that same magazine."

Alfred King was astounded and flashed a broad smile. "How marvelous. I am seldom amazed anymore in my old age, but I admit to you that I am impressed. In answer to your second question, Ole, I come to your village with a profound request. I would like to take Koro to America with me... to be my son or grandson. I have no other family. He would be treated as my own. He has expressed the desire to go with me."

Now it was the tall Maasai's turn to be astonished. "This is a profound and rather stunning request, my friend. You will have to approach Monduli with such a request. He is the chief of *Ilpayiani*, our Maasai Elders. They provide counsel to our village and make the important decisions."

Ole turned to Koro. "Will you show Anwar to my hut please, Koro. Give him a cool drink of honey beer and then show him around our *kraal*."

Then he addressed the white haired, white skinned American. "Come, Mr. King. We will approach the hut of Monduli."

The old Elder, Monduli was squatting on his haunches in front of his hut, enjoying the sunlight. His face was wrinkled and dry like tree bark. He was hairless and toothless. His eyes were dull and milky white. Alf observed immediately that he was blind.

"He does not see. Am I correct?" whispered Alfred King.

"Yes. Glaucoma," answered Ole. "You have noticed the filth in our village, I am sure. Flies by the thousands. Cow dung everywhere. Our huts are even made of cow dung: woven willows smeared with a mixture of mud and cow dung. They are cool in summer heat and warm when the nights grow cold. They serve our purpose, but bring flies and disease. Mr. King, the reason I stay with my people is to attempt to teach them hygiene, health practices and improvement in sanitary conditions. But tradition is difficult to change. My people live today, basically, the same as they lived thousands of years ago."

"Tradition is hard to change anywhere, my friend," said Alfred King. "Even in my own country that thinks it is so civilized and advanced. But I admire you for remaining with your people where your learning can be of most help, although with your education you could be living a much easier life elsewhere."

CHAPTER 4

Ole switched to his native Maasai language. "Old one, Monduli, wise friend, may we sit with you for some talk? I have with me a white man from America, far across the waters. His name is Alfred King. He comes with a rare request."

The old man spoke with a gravely high pitched voice. Ole interpreted for both men. "Yes, please sit. I will welcome your conversation. King... King," he repeated the white man's name. "The name can mean a title, or if not a title, it is one who has power for either good or evil."

Ole and Alf squatted by the old Maasai, which was the customary stance for discussions. Alf's knee bones cracked and popped as he haunched down, not being used to this difficult position. He wondered if he would be able to get up again. "I hope the power of my name is always used for good," he said.

"The white man answers with wisdom," chuckled Monduli. "What is the request you come with, King?"

"I wish to take the boy, Koro, with me to America and make him as my own grandson, as he now is to you. I have no other family. The boy has expressed the desire to go with me."

When Ole interpreted this, Monduli was silent for perhaps two minutes before replying. Voices of children playing could be heard. Women laughed as they went about their tasks. Cattle, goats and domesticated brds all made their contented sounds.

Finally the old blind Maasai spoke. "It is a grave and important request that you make. Koro is important to our village. He is a *Laibon*, one with special powers. He hears sacred and mystical music that no one else hears. It is his gift from The-One-Of-Many-Colors to guide his life. He says that the music comes from another world. I think perhaps it comes from the ancestors. But it matters not because it is a sacred gift.

"One time his music led him to find one of the old grandmothers who had become sick and fallen down in the bushes when we were moving our village to new water and fresh grasses. Another time his music awakened him when a lion had found its way into our *kraal*. He sounded a warning and our warriors chased the beast away. There have been many such incidents. So you see... a gift." He pondered awhile and then added wistfully, "And he is very important to me personally. He has been my eyes, my ears, my joy, most of his young life."

"I am well aware of this, wise old Elder," said the American. "I do not make this request lightly. I could learn much more of life from the boy, and hopefully, he could learn from me. I would protect him with my life." Then he added, profoundly. "And he would be given the freedom to follow his music."

Ole kept opinions to himself except to continue to interpret for these two old men from very different worlds.

"Tell me, King. Are you a man of religion?" asked Monduli.

"I attach myself to no specific religion, although I have worshipped in chapels all over the world. I call myself a Christian and try to abide by Christian morality. I see myself as a spiritual man. I believe in God, probably the same One that you call The-One-Of-Many-Colors or The Giver."

"And what do you do in your land of America to provide for your sustenance?"

Ole interjected. "He wishes to know your occupation or job. How do you earn your living?"

"I raise cattle."

The old Maasai sat up straighter, suddenly alert. His eyes almost seemed to see for a moment. "Ahhhh, yes. That is good. One who raises cattle knows of the earth, the grasses, the weather: sun, rain, dust. He is closer to the Sky Father and the Earth Mother. You, of course, know that our cattle are our very life. Since you are a man of cattle, I will say for your ears to hear one of our major prayers."

He cleared his throat and spit upon the ground, then began, as Ole interpreted each line of the short prayer:

> *"We address You, One-Of-Many-Colors:*
> *Give us children*
> *Give us cattle*
> *Give us rain*
> *Thank You, Giver."*

Tears came to the white man's eyes and overflowed down his cheeks. He could not speak for some time. He dared not tell this humble man that he had become very wealthy from his own cattle. They meant money to him whereas the Maasai cattle meant life to the people, their survival.

"Thank you for sharing your prayer with me, Monduli," was all he could manage to say.

The three of them sat in reverent contemplation.

"Tell me, King," the old Maasai said, after awhile. "The boy might meet fearful situations in your country from being *different*. Is this not so?"

"Yes, that is true. He may be confronted with what is known as prejudice. But perhaps his music can guide him through these tests. Maybe he will become stronger because of them."

"You speak wisely, my white friend. You have convinced me to present your request to our council of *Ilpayiani*. We will meet tonight and our Elders will decide and you must abide by their decision."

He spoke to Ole. "You will show King around our village. He will eat with us. He will sleep tonight in my hut with myself and the boy Koro, so that I might perceive of his true spirit. The driver of the vehicle they came in can abide with you, Ole. And thank you for bringing our talk together for both of our ears and minds to understand."

CHAPTER 5

Night came rapidly near the equator. One minute it was daylight and then suddenly night. Both times were of equal hours, never changing. They all sat around the cooking fire eating hot steaming soup from gourd bowls. Other family groups sat around their fires eating also.

"This is delicious," said Alfred King. "What is it?"

"It is our special soup for guests," replied Ole, smiling. "It is composed of goat milk, calf blood, pieces of cow stomach and slices of meat, flavored with a plant found along rivers, much like our onions. Do the ingredients not make your stomach flip-flop, Mr. King, now that I have revealed them?"

"Not at all, Ole," said the old white man, returning the smile. "My stomach has been conditioned through many varied foods on my travels around the world. I savor foods of different peoples. It is one of my pleasures in travel."

"Then you may wish to thank the woman who has prepared our meal when you have finished. She is standing over there waiting for your approval. Her name is Loiyan."

"I will be sure to thank her."

They finished the meal by drinking honey beer from a gourd and passing it around. The night took on a chill, as cool as the day had been hot. Although near the equator, because of the altitude, nights were cool enough for jackets and blankets for sleeping. Soon after the meal everyone began to go to their huts.

Alfred King and Koro were to sleep on mats upon the ground. Old Monduli was brought in later by some of the Elders of the tribe. They had evidently finished the council meeting for the decision. The white man knew it would not be polite to ask. He must wait until morning to hear the decision. Also, as excited as Koro was, he too must wait. Monduli rolled his mat out upon a bed of piled up sticks and leaves so it wasn't as difficult for him to get up and down.

Sleep came hard for the white haired old American. He worried over whether he was doing the right thing regarding the boy Koro. He was such a little fellow. Then he pondered his own past life, especially the years since his wife had died slowly of cancer. He had cared for her needs tenderly as she died gradually over three years. And then the sudden untimely death of his only child, his handsome, joyful son who died while still in his teens learning to fly an airplane. Alfred had almost given up on life at that time. He had actually wished that he could die also and go wherever it was that his wife and son had gone. But God would not take him. Why? Was he any good to anyone anymore?

What had he accomplished since the deaths of his loved ones? Had he accomplished anything really worthwhile besides raising cattle and making money? Oh, he had contributed large sums to charitable organizations and many worthy causes. He had provided jobs for several people through his many holdings. He had paid for the college educations of two Navajo boys and a Hopi girl, and had put a brilliant boy from a poor family through medical school.

Then he had started his world travels to forget his sorrowing over death, to learn of the peoples and places of our planet earth, perhaps to seek God or to search for meaning in his life. But was there meaning to his life? Who would miss him and mourn over him when he left? Would he leave a dent in the earth that mattered?

These were thoughts and questions that sped through his mind as he tossed and turned upon the sleeping mat.

Koro, the Maasai boy, on the other hand, tossed and turned with excitement, the anticipation of adventure if he were to be allowed to go to a new home in America.

Age and youth—perhaps these were universal differences in

their thinking.

In their tossing and turning, age and youth bumped each other, knocking down the *esos*, which is a woven mat hanging to separate human from animal sleeping quarters. It startled the two baby goats who started bawling so loud that it woke people in the nearby huts. Some came running to see what had caused the commotion.

Koro sleepily explained the mishap. Everyone laughed joyfully at what seemed to them a very funny incident. Then they all went back to their huts and everyone went to sleep, including the perpetrators of the event, Alfred King and Koro.

CHAPTER 6

Next morning, after a breakfast of dried meat, goat's milk and a hard baked bread, Ole came to the hut of old Monduli. He had been at the night meeting of the *Ilpayiani* and knew of the decision of the Elders.

"I have been summoned by the old one here," said Ole, squatting down. "Monduli will now give you the decision of the Elders made in the boy's behalf. I will again talk for you both."

Monduli was squatting, wrapped in his best blanket of red, yellow and brown. Koro was on one side of him and Alfred on the other. Ole sat in front facing them. The old, blind Maasai wet his lips with his tongue. Ole interpreted.

"I have felt of your spirit, King," he began. "And I have determined that you are of a good heart. Words are one thing, but the speaking of your heart and spirit tells me of what are inside of you. I have determined that your heart and spirit are both honest and kind. These are necessary. These are the important factors."

A tear rolled out of his blind eyes. "It has thus been decided that you may take the boy known as Koro with you across the big waters to your own land." His voice trembled, as he added. "And you must give him love."

Alfred King's voice also became emotional, and again, beyond his control, tears overflowed his eyes. "I promise you, Monduli, that I will be his grandfather and give him a grandfather's love."

Ole broke the spell. "Mr. King, do you have paper and pen?"

"Yes. In the van is a notebook and writing equipment."

"Good. Would you please retrieve it. I will draw up the permission given by the tribal Elders and the agreement with you. I will sign it and have each Elder place his mark. This you will need to present to the authorities in Nairobi to get the official documents allowing you to take the boy out of the country and also to permit him to enter into your country."

When Alf came back with pen and paper, he saw old Monduli hugging Koro. Tears flowed from his unseeing eyes. It suddenly struck the American that this old Maasai probably saw more of the things that can't be seen with mortal eyes than men with sight would ever see.

The document was finished and all of the council Elders of the tribe had placed their mark of approval upon it. Ole had written and signed it in English. It stated simply that his Maasai clan, as guardians of the boy called Koro (his full name was written in parenthesis), had agreed to let him go with Alfred King to his home in America and become his grandson by adoption.

Ole handed the paper to Alfred King and waited while he went over and hugged Monduli, then he walked with him, Koro and Anwar out of the *kraal* to the van. He shook hands with Alf and Anwar, then picked up the boy and lifted him high above his head as they both laughed joyfully.

"Will you miss seeing me, Koro?" he asked setting the boy down on the ground.

"Yes, I will, Ole. When I learn to write American as well as you have taught me to speak it, I will write you long letters about my life in America."

"I will look forward to receiving your letters. And remember that Mr. King is now your grandfather. Obey him and treat him with the same respect that you have given to Monduli and the old ones of our tribe."

"I promise to do that, Ole."

Ole turned to Alfred King. "Before you leave, Mr. King, would you tell me what your impressions, your memories of our country will be."

"Of course the animals who roam free and wild," replied the white haired American. "The thousands of wild beasts, gazelles, impala, zebra, and stately giraffe, the elegant ostrich, the elephants, cheetah, lions, leopards, rhinoceros, hippos, colored birds. And the land, the every changing land... from dust a foot deep to waist high grass of the plains, to the lush green of the Great Rift Valley, to the jungles and rivers and lakes with the thousands of flamingoes. And the most marvelous sunrises and sunsets in the world. Majestic Mount Kilimanjaro rising from the plains to its nineteen thousand foot snow capped peak. And Mt. Kenya and Meru. But mostly my memories will be of your peoples, your many tribes who live in peace, who love all children and respect the old among you. These shall be my memories, my friend."

"You speak well in summarizing our country, Mr. King, for these are the things that I treasure also. Now I wish you fair skies and smooth journey."

"Has the boy no belongings?" asked King.

"No. Nothing. Here is a talisman, the old one, Monduli gives to him to remember us by and to protect him. Give it to him when you arrive at your home." He placed in the American's hand a beaded necklace with a polished greenstone figure hanging from it. The figure looked like a replica of a fetus, an unborn child.

Anwar, King and Koro climbed into the van. Many of the tribe had lined up to see The-Boy-Who-Hears-Music leave their village. Everyone waved and Anwar pulled out in a cloud of dust. They were headed toward the big city of Nairobi.

CHAPTER 7

It would be two weeks before the papers could be processed and approved to take the boy Koro out of Kenya. Alfred King paid off his driver Anwar and gave him a gracious bonus. They had grown close during their many weeks of travel together. Anwar had taught King some Swahili language, which was the language most commonly used in these East African countries. In turn, Alf had taught his driver a lot more English than he had known. He also gave Anwar his safari hat.

They embraced and parted, leaving the old American and the Maasai boy alone in Nairobi. The first order of business was to find a hotel, then get some clothes and a travel bag for Koro, then file for the official papers on the boy and try to rush them through.

The hotel they found was one of the nicer ones reserved for tourists and foreign visitors. Koro had never slept in a bed and jumped up and down on it like a trampoline until his little legs collapsed and he fell asleep. Being weary from their long trip, they both slept soundly.

Koro had also never seen a bath or shower. He got under the shower first thing in the morning and stayed under the warm spray for a half hour until Alf finally pulled him out to go down to the coffee shop for a hardy breakfast.

"What kind of clothing would you like?" asked Alf, as they washed their breakfast down with milk.

"Do I get any kind I want?"

"Anything you want that we can find in a store."

"Then I would like the pants that your cowboys wear. I think they are called levis. And I would like a red shirt because that is a color the Maasai people like."

"Okay," said Alfred King. "Let's go see if we can find them."

. . .

The big jet roared down the runway. The pilot gave it full power and it lifted steeply into the sky. It was an overcast day. The airplane flew through thick clouds for awhile and then burst suddenly into bright sunshine and blue sky. Passengers sitting closest to them sneaked curious glances at the white haired, white skinned old man and the small black boy with the big cowboy hat.

During their stay in Nairobi they had visited most everything of interest. They had found a store that sold western goods and Alf bought Koro his levis, a red shirt and a white cowboy hat. They couldn't find boots small enough so settled for Adidas running shoes.

Koro had asked if he would see some cowboys in America and Alfred told him that some worked for him on his ranch and that he would see them every day, even eat with them. They would be his friends and just like family. The boy became so excited that he had jumped up and down with joy.

Knowing the boy had never seen an airplane, let alone flown in one, he leaned over to Koro and asked, "Are you afraid of flying, being so high in the sky?"

Koro had a window seat and had been looking out at all of the clouds below them. "Oh no. I do not fear. Old Monduli taught me how to fly to my music in my dream world. He taught me much magic that was taught to him by the older ones, from the far back in the night of time. I have flown to many places that my music has taken me, but not in airplanes. Just flying free when my mind leaves my body."

"What places?" asked Alf, looking intently at this strange, unusual boy that he had taken to be his own.

"Just different places," was all he would say.

They were quiet for a long time, listening to the drone of the jet engines, the boy staring out of the porthole.

"Alf, those clouds look like other worlds," the boy commented. "I imagine people living in them... do you believe in other worlds that we know nothing about?"

"Yes, I surely do. In our Christian holy book of scriptures, the great God who created all things, the same one you call The Giver, or The-One-Of-Many-Colors, speaks of other worlds. He tells us in the book that He has created worlds without end. That's more worlds than you or I could count or even imagine."

"I believe that, Alf. I sure do believe that." He thought about something, wondering whether to say more, then decided that he could trust his new grandfather completely. "My people, the Maasai, believe that our spirits live forever. Just our bodies die. The ancestors' spirits return. They talk to our shamans and elders of our tribes. I believe all of that, but I also believe some differences."

"What differences?"

"My people, and most people, think all the time about the world after death. The great mystery beyond. But I think and wonder about the world before..."

"Before what, Koro?" Alfred King asked, puzzled.

"The world before we came to this one, Alf. The world our spirits lived in before we were born into this one. We came from somewhere to get to here. That world before we came here. That is the world I think about." He thought some more, and added, "That is where my music comes from, I think."

"A strange and mystical boy. Strange indeed," thought Alfred King. "He has a mind far beyond his years, a mind that reaches out to the past and the future."

CHAPTER 8

They were flying on Alitalia, the Italian airline, and would land at Rome for refueling and have a day and a night layover. The airline put them up in a hotel. King rented a driver and an open carriage pulled by two beautiful black horses. They would tour the ancient and modern sections of the famous city. Koro was so excited he could hardly sit still. His enthusiasm rubbed off on the old man.

"My first real horses," shouted the boy. "I love horses. I have only seen them in pictures. Many animals I have seen, but not horses. They are so wonderful, Alf. You can touch them with your hands. You can feed them. You can ride upon them I have heard it said. And they can pull people in this rolling thing like they are pulling us. Aren't horses grand, Alf?"

"They are indeed, Koro. I am glad that you like them because I have many of them at our ranch that will be your new home."

"You have horses of your very own?" he asked incredulously.

"Yep."

"Could I perhaps sit upon them and learn to ride them?"

"I think so. Although you are still small, some fine cowboys work for me. They can teach you many things about horses and ranching the way we do it in America."

Koro couldn't believe his good fortune. He wanted to see, hear, touch, smell, learn everything so new and different to him. They pulled up near the coliseum. He rubbed his hands on one of the horses as he walked by it.

"This ancient structure is hundreds of years old. It was built when the Roman empire was at its greatest power," Alfred explained, as they walked up the path to enter one of its levels.

"What was it used for?"

"It was used for entertainment of the emperor and other roy-alty and wealthy Romans. They put Christians on the field down there and then turned wild lions loose upon them to watch them fight one another. The Christians most often lost and were eaten by the lions."

Horror shone in the boy's eyes. "They were entertained by watching lions eat people? Why would anyone do that to other people?"

"Because of their religion, what they believed. The Romans did not like the people who were called Christians and who be-lieved in Jesus Christ. This Jesus claimed to be the Son of God who dwelt in the Kingdom of Heaven. The Romans nailed Jesus to a cross and killed him. But after three days lying dead in a tomb, he arose and was alive again. No one had ever done this before, not Buddha, not Mohammed, not Confucius. None of the great religious leaders had risen from the dead. None of them claimed to be the Son of God. So this frightened the Roman lead-ers. They thought that those Christians would take over the power of Rome and put this Jesus on the Emperor's throne. But Jesus said that His kingdom and His father's kingdom was not of this world. It was in another world beyond our sight. So the Romans tried to kill off the Christians.

The boy was thinking. He was quiet as they walked around this ancient amphitheater. He shook his head as if trying to shake out bad thoughts. "How terrible," he said quietly, after much think-ing. "How very bad that people should do that to other people... I have heard much talk about religion. I don't know about religion. What is it, Alf? What is religion?"

"Well, I've never been much on religion myself, Koro, so maybe you are asking the wrong person. But to put it as simple as I can, religion is something that you believe in, something more power-ful than yourself that you worship."

"Like my people, the Maasai, worship The Giver, The-One-Of-Many-Colors?"

"Yes. Like that."

The boy thought again. "I don't think that I have religion, Alf. Is it bad to not have religion? Would it be bad for me?"

"No. I suppose it wouldn't be bad." Then the old man added wisely. "But I think that everyone should have something good to believe in. Perhaps someday you will acquire religion."

"I will think about that," said the boy.

They were back in the carriage touring through many areas of the City of Light. They stopped at a sidewalk restaurant. The driver ate with them. Alfred ordered spaghetti and meatballs and milk for himself and the boy. The driver had lasagna and beer. The boy looked a long time at this strange dish that looked like worms, before venturing to try it. He watched the old man eat his.

"Try it, Koro. I think you will like it. You will eat many new kinds of food in your new life."

Next, Alfred King instructed the driver to take them to the church where the statue of Moses was housed. Koro had eaten every bit of his spaghetti and said he had liked it after all. After Moses, they would visit the Vatican.

. . .

They stood in awe before the sculpture of Moses.

"It was made by a famous sculptor, Michelangelo. He carved it from a solid piece of hard stone called Carerra marble from the place Carerra here in this country of Italy," Alfred instructed Koro. "I have been here many times and find myself more entranced each time I view the magnificent art of Michelangelo. His other works of the David and Pieta are also marvelous. We will go next to the Vatican where you will see some of his painting."

"It is hard for my mind to understand how one man could make that out of stone," said the boy. "The Giver must have liked him a lot to have given him this gift."

They walked around the huge sculpture, viewing it from different angles, watching shafts of sunlight play upon it.

"Who was this Moses," asked the boy, "to have his likeness be so honored?"

"Moses was a great leader of a people called Israelites who lived hundreds of years ago. He led them out of captivity by the Pharaoh in Egypt. He went up to a high mountain where God talked to him and wrote ten commandments upon stone tablets for the people to follow."

"Commandments? Why did the people need to be commanded, Alf?"

"They kept going astray and doing bad things. These ten commandments God gave to them told them what they should and shouldn't do. The Christians even today are supposed to follow the ten commandments, but I fear that too many do not, or the world would be in better conditions."

The boy thought about this. "I don't know about commandments. Can't the people know what is right and do it without being commanded?"

"I surely wish that all people could. But greed for wealth and greed for power and other things often tempt us to do other things... Come. We have other things to see before dark."

. . .

They stood in the center of Vatican Square. The old man was pointing out the statues of the Saints and holy people that circled the Vatican quarters. He pointed

to a window above them. "That is where the Pope lives. He rules Christians called Catholics, all over the world..."

"Rules them? Does that mean that he is like a chief or king?"

"Well I suppose he would be something like a chief. But he is only their religious leader. He tells them what is right for them and what is wrong for them in their religion."

The boy thought long and hard again. "Alf, I don't know about this thing religion. I don't understand why people need to be commanded and ruled. Maybe I need religion and maybe I don't. I think for now I will worship the sky."

"The sky!" exclaimed Alfred King, very interested in the reasoning of this small Maasai boy.

"Yes. I think I will for now worship the sky. It is free without being ruled. It reaches out to forever. It has in it the sun that gives us our daylight. It carries the moon and stars at night. On summer days it sometimes has white clouds that sail peacefully along pushed by the wind that cannot be seen. On some days it turns gray and sends down rain to make things live and grow. So for now I think I will worship the sky."

The old man was again astounded by the profound thinking of the boy who heard music. He hastened to add: "That sounds fine to me, but perhaps there is someone or something greater than sky, sun and moon, maybe someone who created all of those wonders in the sky."

"You mean perhaps the Giver?"

"Perhaps."

"I will think about that," said Koro.

They entered the Vatican and visited the Cistine Chapel, and marveled again at the paintings on the ceiling.

"And this same Michelangelo made all of these colored pictures?" asked Koro in wonderment.

"Yes, he did."

"The Giver must have loved that man to give him those gifts to make beauty for people's pleasure."

On the way back to their hotel, darkness came and the lights of the city came on. Koro's eyes looked everywhere. He could hardly believe what he had seen and was seeing. "Alf, I thank you for this day," he said. "I am learning so much that my thoughts are spinning rapidly inside of my head. Our world is so big and there is so much to see and learn that I will never learn it all."

"No one will, my boy. I have spent the last thirty years trying to see and learn some of it and haven't even scratched the surface."

Koro rubbed his hands on the horses while Alfred King paid the driver.

The next morning the old man found the boy curled up asleep

on the floor. He gently shook him awake. Koro looked up sheepishly. "I tried the bed and it is much too soft from what I am used to. It is fun to jump on it, but I sleep better on something not so soft. I will have many new things to get used to. Is this not so, Alf?"

"Yes, that is so. But you will adjust. You learn fast. Come, hurry now. We must get dressed and brush the teeth as I showed you. Then let's go get on that airplane for the United States of America. Your new home."

PART II
NEW HOME IN AMERICA

CHAPTER 9

The DC-10 turned west over Salt Lake City, out over the Great Salt Lake glittering below in bright sunlight, then banked again, approaching the runway from the north. Alfred King pointed out to Koro where their ranch was, far to the north end of the lake. It would be about a two hour drive from the airport. In a few minutes the big jet touched gently down at the Salt Lake International Airport.

As they came off the ramp into the terminal, they were greeted by a small, wiry, brown skinned young man. He wore faded blue jeans, a purple and white striped shirt, a large brown cowboy hat and well worn boots. His white teeth beamed from ear to ear in a smile, and his black eyes smiled too. He rushed towards the white haired old man who smothered him in a bear hug. Their affection for one another was obvious.

"Mister King, it is so very good to have you back again," said the young man.

"It is good to be back, Rich. I brought a surprise, a new member of our family. This is Koro, from Kenya, East Africa. Koro, this is Richard Gonzalez. He came to live with me when he was just a little guy like you and is now my number one cowboy. His father is our cook, the best in the country."

The young cowboy stuck out his hand and Koro shook it in the custom he had learned that was how Americans greet one another. "Glad to have you in our family, Koro. I hope you will like us."

"Can you teach me to ride horses and be a cowboy too, Richard Gonzalez?"

"Just call me Rich, okay. Sure, I think I can teach you. What I can't teach you, Mister King can. I think he was born on a horse."

"I have never broken Rich of the habit of calling me Mister King although he has been with me many years."

"I do that out of respect for this man, Koro," the brown skinned cowboy explained. "He hired me when I was a poor, ignorant Mexican kid and now he has made me foreman of his ranch and taught me most everything I know. He hired my father too, like he said, and made him the cook for all of us. He is now a good one. Is that not so, Mister King?"

"Best one around. Everyone calls him Gordo. He won't tell us his real name. You will have to get used to our food, Koro. But soon you will love it."

"Let's go get your bags," said the Mexican cowboy. "The jeep four wheeler is in the parking lot. Then we can be on the road home to the ranch. I think you will like our ranch family, Koro."

"I think I will too. If they are happy fellahs like you, Rich, I will sure like them," said the boy in his open honesty. And Richard Gonzalez and Alfred King laughed their happy laughs.

They were soon out on the open highway headed north away from the Salt Lake City metropolitan area. Richard drove casually, occasionally pointing out interesting sights to the wide-eyed black boy, who was so entranced, that for once he had no questions or comments to make. Old man King was weary, but also pointed out something now and then. He also dozed off intermittently, his head bobbing down to his chest to jolt him awake again.

They drove by corn fields, fruit orchards, hay bailers turning out bales, fields of cows, both holsteins and jerseys, sheep, horses grazing, grain waving in the breeze. On the west was the Great Salt Lake. On the east the Wasatch Mountains, some peaks still showing patches of snow. The mountains. Grand, majestic, wonderful. Koro kept looking at them in awe. He had never seen so many mountains. His country was mostly plains or hills. The big mountains, extinct volcanoes, were Kilimanjaro, Kenya and Meru, and they arose alone from the flat land.

They came to a town.

"This is it, Koro. Our town. Skeen, Utah," said Alfred King, "Elevation 4,567 feet. Population 6,327. Some churches, schools, stores, gas stations, small emergency hospital, mostly friendly, neighborly type people, fairly tolerant of the differences in each other. Mostly made up of farm and ranch folks. Our ranch is six miles farther north. All in all not a bad place to live, is it, Rich?"

"Best place I ever been, Mister King."

A few more minutes and Richard Gonzalez announced, "Here we are. Home. King Cattle Ranch. Best in the west."

They drove up a long gravel driveway with white four rail fences on both sides, leading to a long rambling brick ranch house. There was another house back farther and to the side. There were also several other buildings: a large shed for machinery; a barn for milk cows; a long row of chicken coops; a hay and grain storage barn and several smaller sheds. Shady maple and elm trees surrounded the ranch house, and on the front lawn an elegant weeping willow presided. Cattle could be seen in all directions as far as eyes could see.

"This is it, Koro. Your new home."

The little black boy's eyes were round as quarters looking at all of the cattle.

"Our cattle are called herefords. Much different from the cattle of your people, Koro."

"Yes, Alf. They are different. I have never seen their kind before."

A big cowboy was entering the ranch house as they got out of the jeep. Two more rode up on horses. Koro noticed that they all took off their boots and hats before entering the house.

"Come on, aren't you two hungry?" asked Richard Gonzalez. "I called my Papa just before we left the airport. Gordo said he would have a big feed ready for us."

CHAPTER 10

A long dining room table was set with seven places. A white linen tablecloth covered the table. Each place was laid out in the finest china, silverware, linen napkins and crystal drinking glasses. They all washed in a large washroom with four wash basins just inside the back entrance, then quietly seated themselves. When Gordo, the cook, finished bringing the food to the table, he took a seat himself. Alfred King, at the head of the table spoke softly.

"Koro, we always say a short prayer before our meals thanking our great God for His gifts. I hope this will be with your approval also."

"Yes, Alf. I like that very much."

Everyone lowered their heads as old man King said, "Our Heavenly Father, we thank You for our friendship one with another. And we thank You for the bounties of life You have given us. Amen."

The cowboys all echoed "Amen."

"Okay, everyone, dig into the food while I introduce our new family member," said Alfred King. "This is Koro, from the country of Kenya in East Africa. I hope you will all make him feel at home with us. I plan to make him officially my grandson as soon as I can contact my attorney, Ed Withers."

The old man King looked proudly at the small black boy. "This means that you will have a second name, Koro, the same as mine. You will be an American, named Koro King."

Everyone applauded, as Koro gave his white-toothed grin. "I will be a good grandson to you, Alf," he said.

"I'm sure you will. Now, around the table I want you to meet your family. This little man is Gordo, greatest cook in the west.

He is Richard's Papa. Next is the biggest and oldest at the ripe old age of thirty-one, Larry, from the state of Montana. Chuck is the short one with all of the muscles. He is from Colorado. The tall skinny feller, tough as rawhide, is Dex, from Wyoming. This is your new family, Koro. What do you think?"

"I am happy to be here in America with you," said the little black boy. "I hope that you will all teach me to be a good cowboy too. And I hope you will all like me."

They all laughed and everyone started talking at once. The Maasai boy seemed to put a new spark of life in them. Koro added an afterthought. "Never have I seen such a big house. And never have I seen so much food to eat. This would feed my whole tribe for many days."

They chuckled again, enjoying the exuberance of this happy little guy.

"These rowdy fellows used to eat at the bunkhouse, but I decided to teach them manners. We eat upon the best plates with the best utensils and finery you can find in any dining room. I figure if they learn proper etiquette they might just be able to catch them a wife some day. Big Larry has himself a girl in town. It might just turn serious. Who knows."

Larry turned a bright pink, his usual shy reaction.

"Watch how these fellows handle their eating equipment and you will soon catch on," continued Alfred King. He knew how to set people at ease. "They can teach you a lot of things, and I believe you will teach them also."

They finished eating and talking. Dex helped Gordo carry dishes to the kitchen and clean up the table. They passed the assignments around each week.

"Bedtime. Big day ahead," announced the King, as they sometimes affectionately called the old man. He showed Koro down the hall to his room and pointed out the closest bathroom.

"Wow! This is a mighty big room. A whole family of my people in Kenya could live in it," he said as he jumped happily on the hug, soft bed.

Early next morning, the King came to wake up the boy Koro and found him curled up asleep on the floor again. At first the little Maasai didn't know where he was and was disoriented. Then he was once more embarrassed to be found on the floor.

"I am really sorry, Alf," he said when finally awake. "You have given to me such a fine, soft bed and I can't use it for sleep. I have a request to make if you will hear it."

"Sure, let's hear it," said the old man, stifling a laugh.

"If you would give me permission to sleep in the bunkhouse with the cowboys, maybe their bunks might be hard as my ground bed in Kenya and I can sleep."

"That sounds like a reasonable request. I will let you sleep in the bunkhouse until school starts this fall; then you must sleep here so that you can study your lessons. Okay with you?"

"That will be okay. I will study well in school so I can write letters to Ole. And I will learn to sleep in soft bed then."

"Agreed. Let's go to breakfast now, and afterwards I will give you your first ride on a horse with me."

. . .

Koro wore his red shirt, blue jeans and white cowboy hat. Alf sat him on the saddle in front of him. They rode out east toward the mountains. Cattle roamed everywhere they looked. The morning sun sparkled like diamonds on the Great Salt Lake far out to the west.

"This is a most wonderful time for me, Alf, to be upon a horse. Old Monduli would laugh with pleasure to see me now," Koro shouted excitedly.

"We'll have to go into town and get you some boots if you're going to be a real cowboy."

"Why do you keep so many cattle?" the boy questioned.

"We raise them from when they are calves. We fatten them up and then sell them to the market. That is how we make money to live. Here in America people seem to need money. Americans eat lots of beef: roasts, prime rib, steaks, hamburgers. You will see how we eat lots of meat."

"My people eat meat of cattle also and we drink their blood and their milk. But we do not sell them for money. The cattle are our wealth. We keep them for our tribe."

"I know you do, and often I think your way is better. But you will find that many things are different here, and perhaps, sadly, most everything revolves around money."

They rode through beautiful range land and more cattle, silent for a long while. The boy kept looking at the lofty mountains and the many red and white cattle, trying to comprehend it, to take it all in.

"Are you sorry you brought me here, Alf?" he asked suddenly. "You treat me so fine and buy me things. Then I can't sleep on nice bed. And I ask lots of questions. Are you wishing you had left me in Kenya?"

"Not at all, my son. Don't ever think that. I am very happy that you have come here to live with me. We can learn much from each other."

"Thank you, because I am happy even if I miss my people." He thought awhile and added. "I have thought much about this religion thing and have decided for now to pray, as you call it, each night to the Giver. I don't need to ask for children or cattle or rain as Monduli did. There are plenty of those here in America. I think that I will ask The Giver to send upon us love."

"That sounds like a fine idea," said the white haired old man, smiling to himself.

. . .

Alfred King went to the bunkhouse that night to take the boy some bedding. He heard him entertaining the cowhands with stories of his homeland, and he couldn't help himself from stopping outside the door to listen.

"Are you sittin' there meaning to tell me that the houses you lived in were made of cowpies?" asked Dex from Wyoming.

"It is quite true," replied Koro. "What you call cowpies, we know as cattle dung or the fresh droppings of our cattle."

"Yuk!" said Chuck from Colorado, pulling a contorted face.

"I will tell you how we make our houses," continued the boy Koro. "I helped make them many times. We gathered long sticks and willows. We placed one end into the ground and bend them over." He demonstrated. "Then many willows are tightly woven, then we smeared the mixtures of mud and cow dung, making them sealed for the weather. Inside they are cool when weather is hot, and warm when weather is cold."

"Don't they stink?" asked Chuck.

"Not when you grow up used to them. We often had to move to new areas for water and grass for our cattle. Our houses we left behind would wash away and disappear when rainy season came. Then new grass would grow where our houses once stood. Nice way, huh?"

"Amazing," remarked Larry, the big bashful cowboy from Montana.

"On the way here Koro told me about their cattle," said Rich Gonzalez. "Tell them how your cattle are different from ours," he requested of the enthused Maasai boy.

"Our cattle are many different colors. They have long ears, loose skin under neck. Some have long horns and hump on shoulders."

"Brahma's," cut in Dex. "Mean critters. I rode one once in a rodeo in Laramie."

"And you don't have horses to herd them with and round them up?" questioned Chuck.

"No horses," said Koro. "We have some donkeys, but I never see a horse in my country."

"Then how do you watch the herd, take care of them, you know?" continued Chuck questioning.

"Our warriors stand all day and watch them so lions and hyenas don't kill them..."

"Amazing," said Larry again.

"Your warriors stand on their feet all day long and just watch the cattle?" asked Dex.

"That is true. We learn to stand on one leg like the pink flamingo bird, and change to other leg when tired. They hold spear also to kill wild beasts that attack herd."

Koro demonstrated how the warriors put one foot up on the other knee to stand on one foot. His audience watched attentively.

Alfred King walked in with the bedding.

"Ah, Mister King, Koro was telling us stories of his people and cattle," explained Rich Gonzalez. "Sit awhile. My Papa is ready to play his guitar for us."

"Thank you. I believe that I will sit awhile. Here is the boy's bedding. You can show him later how to make up a bunk bed."

The little Mexican cook, Gordo, brought out a large Spanish guitar and began to pick and strum beautiful music. Koro's eyes grew wide. His ears perked up. He loved the music. After awhile they all started singing old cowboy songs and some Mexican songs. They sang late into the night. Finally, white haired old King excused himself.

"I hate to leave, but I grow weary with my many years. I ought to bunk here with you fellows instead of alone in that big house."

Just before they turned lights out, Koro told them how he had enjoyed the music. He spoke of the music that he heard from another world. He spoke of how it guided his path in this world. He told them that his people had made him a *Laibon*, one with special powers because of his music, and that they called him The-Boy-Who-Hears-Music. He told them all of this because he considered them to be his people, his brothers.

The cowhands looked at him strangely.

CHAPTER 11

The long days of summer were becoming shorter as they headed toward autumn. After a long battle, Koro had finally become the adopted grandson of Alfred King, mainly because of the reputation and influence of old King and also the expertise of Ed Withers, his long time friend and attorney. It was argued by the adoption court that Alfred King was too old and that the boy would not have a mother figure and just be around a bunch of rowdy cowhands. But Ed Withers pointed out that the boy had had no mother in Kenya and was being raised by an equally old man named Monduli along with other Elders of the tribe. So the legal adoption was granted and the boy became Koro King on the official records.

Next a birth certificate was obtained from the Bureau of Records and Statistics. His exact birth date was not known, so he was given a birthday the same day as his adoption and was made to be eight years old. Koro King, eight year old Kenya Maasai, now a small American cowboy.

He still wore gold earrings. His hair was growing out and was very curly. He was gradually becoming Americanized, wearing boots, hat and jeans quite naturally. And with hard work and good food he had already grown several inches.

Old man King had given him a horse, which he had learned to bridle, saddle and ride with some skill. Koro had become like a little brother to the cowhands and other workers at King Cattle Ranch. He was especially fond of Rich Gonzalez, the young Mexican foreman, and rode with him every day. Rich had taught him of equipment and lingo of the horseman: saddle, halter, ackamore, bridle, martingale, spurs, chaps, quirt, stirrups. He was learning to cut out cattle to be branded or dehorned, and how to rope calves. He loved it all.

But Alfred King was his guardian, master, mentor and god. He practically worshipped the white haired old gentleman who had brought him to this land of milk and honey and given him this new life of boundless opportunities.

On a day of blue sky and bright sun, when the work was caught up and most hands had a day off, Koro, who had been sitting on the lawn looking longingly at the mountains to the east, made a sudden request of old King.

"Alf, will you walk with me up those mountains?"

"We call that hiking, my boy. I don't know if my old legs will carry me. But what the heck, let's give it a go. Tell you what. We'll go on an overnighter. I'll get Gordo to pack up some grub and we'll take our bedrolls and sleep up in those mountains. How does that sound?"

"That will be a great thrill and pleasure for me, Alf."

Mountains have long been a fascination for mortals. They were the dwelling place of the mythical Greek gods and goddesses, and they have been sacred spots to many native peoples and religions of the world. Many climb their summits to worship or to seek solace. Others do so as a challenge or a feat to be accomplished. Many climbers, such as those who have climbed the highest peak, Mount Everest, speak of having conquered it... where in reality, a mountain is never conquered. A mountain is forever, majestic, mysterious. Philosophers through the ages have referred to the everlasting hills and mountain peaks as holy, the footstools of the Almighty.

To Alfred King, mountains signified peace, a comfort, something that could always be relied on. They were constant. Always there. He could not imagine living in flat country. To Koro King, having been raised on the Serengeti Plains of Africa, where the world is flat for hundreds of miles in every direction, mountains presented a new vista of mystery and adventure. He had seen Mount

Kilimanjaro just over the border in Tanzania, but once, and then its peak had been shrouded in clouds.

The tall old white man and the small black boy each carried a pack with a sleeping bag and some food. They soon reached the foothills east and not far from the ranch buildings. King cattle could be seen everywhere, even scattered throughout the foothills. Then they started climbing into the steep rock and scrub oak, following animal trails for easier going.

They reached the summit of the highest peak east of the ranch house by late afternoon, took off their packs and leaned against a big rock to eat their lunch. The rock provided some shade from the sun. Cold water from their canteens quenched their thirst.

"You hike so well for one who carries seventy-five years upon him, Alf," said the boy, after they had sat quietly for awhile. "You would make a good Maasai. Our feet carry us everywhere that we go."

Old King chuckled. "I suppose it's because I have always stayed pretty active and tried to take proper care of my body. But I have to admit that my bones creak a bit more and my muscles tighten up on me a bit. I'll suffer for it tomorrow."

The valley below them was green with crops, and yellow with ripening grain. The town of Skeen was a miniature. The Great Salt Lake glistened in the distance like liquid gold.

"Pretty, isn't it?" remarked Alfred King.

"It is very beautiful," said Koro. "I am so happy that you agreed to hike with me, as you call it."

"So am I, Koro. I had forgotten what it was like, and the fresh feeling it gives. I used to hike all of these mountains when I was a boy. Knew them like the back of my hand."

He paused to drink again from the canteen. Nothing quenched thirst like cold canteen water except water right out of a pure mountain stream. "All of that valley as far as you can see was colonized by a great pioneer and religious leader named Brigham Young," he explained to the boy. "He brought his people, called Mormons, out here to escape religious persecution. Mobs of hoodlums murdered the founder of Mormonism for his beliefs. He was their first prophet—Joseph Smith..."

"They killed a man because of his religion?"

"Yep. Murdered his brother Hyrum along with him while they were supposedly under protection of the law. They didn't see much law in Ohio, Missouri or Illinois. So Brigham Young became their next leader and brought the Mormons out here where there was nothing but sagebrush and prairie dogs. They came in wagons pulled by oxen, and many of them even walked, hundreds of miles, contending with mud, cold, Indians, sickness. Lots of them died on the way and were buried in the prairies. Brigham had seen this place in a vision, so when they came through the canyon and saw this valley he knew it and said, 'This is the place,' and he made a prophecy that his people would make this valley blossom like a rose. And it has come true. That's why most of the people here in Utah are Mormons today."

"I can't understand why people kill others for what they believe, or because they seem different. Can you understand it, Alf?"

"Nope, I can't."

"Sometime, could we perhaps visit a Mormon church?"

"Sure. And several other churches too, since you seem to be interested in religion. That will be something we can do together, and both of us can maybe learn something... now stand up and turn around. Look out to the east. See all of that country, clear out there until it faces into a haze... that's where Dex comes from. That is the state of Wyoming...

"Your continent of Africa is divided into several separate countries. Our continent of America is divided into many states. But we are one country, the United States of America."

"You are teaching me so much, Alf."

"You are a good student, Koro. I dare say that you already know as much as many junior high boys and girls, and you haven't even been to our schools yet.

"Let's get moving down the other side of this mountain. There's a spot I remember as a boy. I want to see if it is as beautiful as I remember it. We can reach it before dark and sleep there tonight. I named it Hidden Valley."

There was a well trodden deer trail down. It soon came alongside of a clear creek, bounding over rocks on its way down into the valley. Soon they entered a different realm in the pine trees.

"Smell those pine trees," said Alf. "Have you ever smelled anything so good?"

"Only Gordo's cooking," replied Koro, and they laughed.

The trail broke free from the pines and entered a small peaceful valley surrounded by quaking aspen trees. The stream smoothed out and ran through the center of the valley and off down a canyon.

"Yep. This is it. My Hidden Valley. I can't believe so many years have passed since I was in this place, and was just a boy like you. Time moves on just like that stream and our lives move with it. That water is never the same from one second to the next and we are never the same person. Always changing."

The sun was below the mountain, headed to the western horizon on its daily journey. The air was fresher, cooler down in Hidden Valley. A breeze rustled the aspens. Birds sang and called to one another. A nois chipmunk scolded the intruders. A few crickets began their syncopated chorus as shadows lengthened.

"Let's unpack and put our sleeping bags out under this big cottonwood tree," said the old man. "Just up here from the stream. Take a drink out of the creek, Koro. The sweetest water you will ever taste."

The boy lay down and drank deeply from the creek. "And the coldest water I ever had too," he remarked. "It freezes the teeth."

Night came fast in the folds of the mountains. They munched on some cookies and crawled into their sleeping bags. There was no moon as yet, so they could see millions of stars through the trees. They talked about many things until late at night when all sounds but the creek ceased. It was a time that drew them close together and neither of them would ever forget.

As the boy looked up at the stars, the last thing he said before his eyes closed in sleep was, "I wonder which one of those worlds my music comes from?"

CHAPTER 12

Autumn was pushing its way into the valley, but Indian summer refused to leave. Colors appeared in the hills: red, yellow, orange, golden hues. Koro King was growing accustomed to his new home and way of life. His jeans and shirt were faded. His hat was dusty and sweat stained. His boots were softened, scuffed and wellworn. He was fully initiated as a cowboy, and rode hard and worked hard with the older cowhands.

His close friend and mentor, Rich Gonzalez, had never attended school, but each night had been tutored over the years by the other literate cowboys. He had learned reading and writing well and devoured books hungrily that Alfred King brought him. Now he and others were teaching Koro reading and writing.

School would be starting in a couple of weeks and he had already learned from his friends Rich, Chuck, Larry and Dex, how to print many words and put some together into sentences. He was so eager to learn that his efforts paid off like magic. He composed his first letter to his former mentor, Ole, in Kenya:

> *My dear friend Ole,*
> *I miss to see you.*
> *Alf King is good man.*
> *I have good friends here.*
> *I will start America skool soon.*
> *Happy, Koro King*

He was placed in third grade at Skeen Elementary School according to his test scores and birth certificate. He was eager and seemed unafraid to enter this new experience. He wanted to walk the six miles into school since he walked everywhere in Kenya, but soon found that riding the school bus was fun, and he met other school kids that way.

On the school bus, friends were made... and enemies. Forty-five kids all talking, arguing, shouting, singing. The bus covered most of the north end of the valley, so Koro got to see many of the little communities, farms and ranches.

The girl got on the bus near the west rim of the valley, near the lake. She was brown skinned with dark eyes and hair, and was older than Koro. "Can I sit here by you?" she asked him.

"Yes. Sure," he said, smiling at her.

"You're new here in the valley, I guess, huh?" she questioned, friendly like.

"I just been here a little while. I live with Alfred King and belong to him now."

"Are you from a big city ghetto? I mean since you are black. Not many blacks around here," she said in a straight forward manner.

"No. I have heard about those ghettoes, but I am from Kenya."

"Where is that?"

"In the country of Africa."

"No kidding," said the girl, surprised. "You are a real honest African, huh?"

"Yes. I am of the Maasai tribe. My name is Koro," he answered proudly.

"No kidding," she repeated. "A real African black. We have something in common. I am from the Ute tribe out in the Uintah-Ouray Reservation. I live here with the Wheelers during the school year and then go back to my tribe for summer. I just got back here last week. My name is Alice Goldtooth."

"You are what is known as Native American? You are the real American of this country?" he asked eagerly.

"Well, yes," she said hesitantly. "You make it sound real neat. Most people just call us Indians and consider us third class citizens. If you just came from Africa, how come you know about Native Americans?"

"I been asking a lot of questions and trying to learn about this great America that will now become my country," said Koro.

"I like that, Koro, and I like you. Most Indian peoples are shy and afraid of white people, but we Utes are different. We speak our mind more. I think that me and you will be good friends. We are both kind of misfit natives."

The bus pulled up in front of the Skeen School. It was the elementary and junior high combined, one in one half of the building and the other in the other half. High school students had to go ten or twelve miles away to the city of Ogden.

An older, square built boy had been staring all the time at Koro from across the aisle, giving him mean looks. As they got off the bus he walked up and said, "I don't like you, dude. My Pa says you Blacks are just plain niggers and that you are no good. So you just better stay out of my way." Then he gave him a shove.

Alice Goldtooth saw it and gave the boy a menacing look. She turned back to Koro and said, "Don't worry about him. He is what we call a bully. His name is Rolly Benson. I'm not afraid of him and he knows it. If he ever gives you any trouble let me know and he'll be sorry."

So on his first school day he had made a good friend and one who, for some reason, didn't like him. He could not understand this. He would have to find out why.

CHAPTER 13

Old King was angry. His face was red. His eyes were flashing. "You say this boy at your school, this Rolly Benson, called you a nigger?"

"Yes, Alf, and he looked at me like hate. What is this nigger word? Why did he call me that?" the small black boy asked innocently.

Alfred King thought for awhile on how best to answer. Also he tried to calm himself and let his anger subside. "It is a word of hate," he finally managed to say. "It is a word of fear, of suspicion, of intolerance. It is what is known as prejudice and bigotry, Koro. I suppose that I was so naive that I thought you wouldn't come up against it here in our peaceful valley. But I was wrong, I can see. It seems that prejudice shows its ugly face in every nook and cranny of our world in one way or another."

The boy looked at him bewildered, not knowing what he was trying to explain. The old man sensed that he wasn't speaking plainly enough for the boy to grasp what he was trying to explain.

"Nigger is a word of hate. Some white people of fear and hate call those with black skin niggers. It means to them that black is not as good as white. It makes these mean, ignorant whites feel that they are superior when they use the word nigger for blacks. They lump them all together and don't even look at them as individuals."

Alfred was getting angry again. "I think we better visit this Rolly Benson's Pa and have a little plain discussion. I have heard of the man. Word is around that he beats the kid and is not a very understanding man."

"No, Alf. I do not want us to go to him. It might bring more hate. Rolly does not know me yet. Maybe I can win him as a friend. Alice Goldtooth, my new friend says that no one likes Rolly. Maybe I can become his friend if I try hard."

Old King let out his breath slowly and looked at his black grandson lovingly. "Perhaps you are right," he said. "You are a more tolerant person than I am. Let's try it your way."

Koro King met another form of what Alf had called prejudice. It was a more subtle form, not full of bitterness and hatred, but a form that hurt a bit because it came from those that he considered to be his brothers, the cowhands. It was a prejudice against children. Perhaps because he was little or young in years. He didn't know why.

In his country in Africa among his own tribe, children and old ones were considered equal or even above those in the middle. People gave children their time. They told them the stories of the ancestors. They passed on to children the myths and legends of their people. They taught them the traditions and customs. They, in turn, listened to the children, heard their ideas and opinions, answered their questions. And they considered their talk important.

Here in America, childrens' opinions didn't seem to matter much. He had told the cowhands about his music, a mystical music that came from another world, music that no one else could hear. He told them how it guided the path that he walked in this world. He told them how in his village he was called The-Boy-Who-Hears-Music because he had this special gift and power. He had seen their raised eyebrows, their sideways smiles and their winks at one another. They figured it was the fantasy or imagination of a child. And he said nothing. He loved them and knew they loved him. But he was just a child to them, a child with childish thoughts.

And then something happened that changed it all. They all became believers... believers in his music... believers in The-Boy-Who-Hears-Music.

CHAPTER 14

Koro King said to Alfred King, "There is something bad to happen today." He was on his way to catch the school bus. He added hesitantly. "My music had a sad melody this morning. I did not wish to say this to any other than you. They would not consider this to be serious. So would you tell our family to be careful and and alert."

Old King had moved the boy back into his room in the ranch house so that he could study school work and get some sleep. He had found him asleep again on the floor and thought he had seemed a bit anxious about something when he had awakened him.

"Yes, I will warn the others to be alert today. Did your music indicate what the trouble might involve?"

"No. Only that something bad is to happen today to one of our family." And he had left for school.

The bully, Rolly Benson, had bumped him every time they passed and called him nigger. Koro paid him no heed but thought to himself that such a boy must be very unhappy. All day his thoughts had been elsewhere and teacher had asked if he was ill. When he arrived back at the ranch his fears left him for a moment, as Alf seemed quite happy. Gordo also sang a pleasant Mexican song as he started to prepare the evening meal.

Koro tried to study his school work in his room but his music still played a disturbing melody. He heard Gordo ringing the dinner bell and went to the washroom where he met the others coming in to clean up for the evening meal. They bantered back and forth jokingly, as always, and asked him how his school work was coming.

Larry said, "Dex must be trying for overtime pay. He hasn't

come in from the range yet."

"That's not like him," said Chuck. "Although he's skinny as a fence post, he always eats enough for two of us."

"Put Dex a meal in the oven to keep warm, Pa," said Rich to Gordo. "He'll be hungry enough to eat hay when he gets in."

They finished eating and were cleaning up the table and still Dex hadn't showed up. They heard a whinny out front and Alf looked out the window. "It's his horse and no Dex. Something has happened to him. We'd all better saddle up and spread out to look for him. That sky looks bad too. Could be an early winter storm moving in."

"Let me go too, Mr. King," said Gordo.

"Okay. Saddle your pa a horse, Rich. You and him can go off east into the foothill area. Larry, you ride down through the flat land toward the lake. Chuck, you head up kind of northwest. I'll just kind of ride around where fate leads me. And I want you all back by dark. If we don't find him, I'll call in a search and rescue helicopter tomorrow."

"Alf, I want to go too." It was Koro, standing back, forgotten for the moment. "I can find him."

"I know you can ride, Koro, but you are still a beginner. And with twilight, the horses can't see as well. It could be too dangerous."

"Alf, I know I can find Dex. My music is pulling me toward him. Remember, I told you this morning something bad would happen?"

The old man suddenly remembered. "By golly, you did warn us. Okay, my boy. Get your horse saddled and you can come with me."

It took him just a few minutes and he rode up beside King.

"All right, Koro, you're the leader for now. Which way do we go?" he asked.

"Straight up there," Koro said, pointing. "The direction you call north."

So the old man and the boy loped off northward toward some

rugged mountains, gullies and ravines. The sun dropped into the Great Salt Lake. The sky became streaks of pink and red, soon turning to gray. The clouds that had been gathering in the north became ominous.

"I think we better head back, Koro," said Alfred, sounding discouraged.

"Not yet, Alf. Just a little more and we be near to where Dex is."

So they rode on until they neared a steep ravine cut into the rocks and sloping down into a canyon that was swallowed up by the encroaching darkness.

"I think he is close by, Alf," said the boy. Then he yelled, "Dex, where are you?"

They heard a faint groan, and then, "Down here. Help! I'm at the bottom down here."

They dismounted their horses and tied them to a scrub oak bush, and began to scurry down the ravine, half sliding on rocks and loose shale. They found him wedged against a large rock, his ankle twisted awkwardly under him.

"How did you ever find me?" he moaned. "I thought I was a goner. My horse stumbled and we rolled clear down here. I think he rolled on me twice. I thought he might have been killed but he got up and took off."

"As to finding you, you can attribute it to Koro's music. He led us right to you."

"Thank the good Lord, and thank you, Koro. No more will I be a doubter. You have made me a true believer in whatever magic you and your music have."

"Where are you hurt most, Dex?" asked Koro, with concern.

"I just hurt, terrible all over," groaned Dex. "But I think I got me some broken ribs and at least a broken ankle. Maybe more. I tried to stand up and couldn't. I tried to crawl and couldn't."

"Well, we're going to have to hurt you some more to get you out of here. There's no other way," said King. "I can lift you up on your feet and grab you around the waist. Then you'll have to use

me and Koro as crutches on each side of you. Koro, you take the
other side and lift... ready,Dex?"

"I'm ready."

"Okay, pal, grit your teeth," said the old man.

Dex screamed in pain as they managed somehow, to half walk
him, half drag him, up the slope and out of the ravine, then get
him up on Alf's horse with the old man sitting behind him and
trying to hold him on. It was dark now. Koro led the way on his
horse with them close behind.

The others were all waiting and had turned on all of the lights
around the ranch to guide them back. "Richard, bring the four
wheeler here," King yelled, when he saw them. "He's hurt pretty
bad. Horse fell on him. We'll drive him to St. Benedict's Hospital
in Ogden. We can get him there as fast as it'll take a helicopter to
get here from Salt Lake."

Richard Gonzalez, Alf, and Koro went in the van with him.
They propped him up with pillows in the back seat. He felt better
sitting up than lying down. "The rest of you get some sleep. We'll
give you a report in the morning. And thanks, all of you," the old
man added, as they drove off into the night. A light snow had
begun to fall. It was November.

CHAPTER 15

Dex returned to the ranch on Thanksgiving. Gordo had prepared an enormous dinner: turkey, ham, roast beef, mashed potatoes, yams, cranberries, corn, beets, you name it. And four kinds of pie: pumpkin, mincemeat, apple, and banana cream. Drink of the day was hot apple cider, seasoned with nutmeg and cinnamon.

Snow was falling and had covered the ground. Koro had played in the cold white stuff all afternoon. It was the first time he had seen it close and felt it. When he saw it once, high on the top of Mount Kilimanjaro, he hadn't imagined that it was cold and fluffy and that you could mold it in your hands.

A fire burned in the huge rock fireplace of the dining room. Everyone felt warm, comfortable, good inside. Dinner was finished and they slid their chairs back for some talk.

"I think we should all give Gordo a round of applause for the best dinner anyone could dream up," said Alfred King.

They all clapped and cheered. Gordo raised both hands in the air and smiled his thanks.

"And I would like to welcome Dex back with us," said Rich Gonzalez. "We are sure all happy to have you here with us again, Dex."

"It's great to be back," said Dex. He was still on crutches. He had broken his ankle and smashed his knee. He had also broken five ribs and punctured a lung. "I suppose I am lucky to be alive. I got me a metal knee cap and screws and bolts in my ankle, so I can now forecast the weather when they act up."

Everyone laughed. Then Dex spoke more seriously. "And I want to acknowledge that I owe my good fortune of being here again with you fellows, to our little brother Koro and what he calls his music. I might still be lying in that gully except for his music. No more will anyone make light of his music or they will answer to this skinny but tough cowboy named Dex. And I suggest that from here on that we think of him, like his people in Africa did, as The-Boy-Who-Hears-Music."

Everyone cheered in agreement. When they quieted down, Koro said, "Will someone tell to me what is this Thanksgiving that we are having. What does it mean?"

They all looked at one another sheepishly, having assumed that this small black boy from a totally different culture would know about Thanksgiving.

"Do the honors of explaining, Larry," said old King.

Larry, oldest of the cowhands and rather shy, coughed a few times gathering his thoughts, and began. "It is a special day, Koro, that one of our former presidents of our country made an official celebration day. It is kind of in memory of when the first white men landed in America and had a peaceful feast with the Indians who were already here. It is a time for us to give thanks to our Creator, the great God, for all of the blessings he has given to us..."

"Just one day?" interrupted Koro. "Why must there be only one day to give our thanks?"

They all looked down at their hands foolishly, as Koro went on. "Among my people, the Maasai, we thank the Giver every day of our lives. There is not just one day of a whole year. We give thanks every day."

Chuck leaned back in his chair, flexed his muscular shoulders and arms and took over for Larry. "Your people are absolutely right, Koro. Thanks should be given every day to our God. There are wars going on all over the world, pain, suffering, and death... people starving, little children hurting. But here in America you have seen how much we have... too much... beautiful houses, cars, television sets, computers. Too much comfort perhaps. Many people in America get greedy for money and more money... and power and authority. Many people forget how much we have. We forget to be thankful. So maybe this Thanksgiving day at least reminds us to be thankful."

"Amen to that, Chuck," added old King. "And now, Gordo, would you bring out your guitar and give us the pleasure of playing for us. And maybe we can loosen up and sing along on some familiar tunes."

They sang, ate second helpings of pie, and talked late into the night. There was a feeling of closeness among them.

CHAPTER 16

"Koro, I've been thinking," said the old man one day in late January. "We are into a new year. When a new year starts here in America, we try to take a new look at things and re-evaluate ourselves, set some new goals. I have come to the conclusion that you need the influence of a woman in your life. All you have around you are a bunch of rough, tough, although kind, cowboys."

"Mostly I just lived with men among my Maasai, Alf."

"I know, but I think that you need to be mothered now and then, and I've got an idea. You see that beautiful grand piano sitting in the living room? No one plays it."

"It is called a pi-an-o?"

"That's right. Piano. A person who knows how to play it can make beautiful music come from it. Since my good wife died, it has sat there silent, a real shame. You, Koro King, will learn to play it and make music come from it once again."

"How can I learn to play it, Alf?"

"There is a lady who lives down the road a piece, about two miles. She is an old widow lady, frail and small as a sparrow, but how she can play a piano. In her younger years she was a famous concert pianist. She once toured the world, playing with some of the great symphony orchestras.

"The boys take turns looking in on her, make sure she has food and medicine and what she needs. They take her to a movie or some special event now and then. She is lonely, but independent. You will be a breath of fresh air for her and she can teach you to play the piano. One of our boys can drop you off at her place two or three times a week when they take the laundry into Skeen, and pick you up on their way back. Then you can practice on our piano here. It will be good to hear music coming out of it again."

"You are saying to me that in your village in Africa that they referred to you as The-Boy-Who-Hears-Music?"

The question was put straight forward to him by his new music instructor upon their first meeting. They were sitting on the piano bench in front of the Steinway grand piano. It was black, and filled most of the small living room. Her entire house was small, suitable for the small Mrs. Leckner. She wasn't too much bigger than her small wide-eyed pupil. She wore her hair pulled back severely and tied in a bun at the back. Her eyes were gray like her hair, but pierced into the eyes of whomever she addressed.

"Yes," he said shyly. "It was a title of honor. The Giver, for some reason, had given me this gift to hear beautiful music..."

"Does this music come from inside of your head or your heart?" she wanted to know.

"No, Missus Leckner, it seems to come from out in the sky, somewhere far away. Maybe from another world. And it seems to pull me, to guide me to someone who needs help, or it is telling me how to walk my path."

She accepted this explanation, thought for awhile, and then asked, "Have you heard of a man named Beethoven?"

"No, I have not heard about that man."

Ludwig Von Beethoven lived many years ago. He was deaf in his mortal ears, but he must have heard music from somewhere because he composed some of the most beautiful music ever written."

He listened intently, hanging on this small woman's every word. She had listened to him like Alfred King had listened to him. She accepted him as someone important. He would learn much from her.

"You see this big shiny piano?" she continued. "I expect that you can learn to make music come out of its keys. Although your legs won't quite reach the pedals yet, I see that you have large hands. Good. One f my favorite pianists is a tall Texan named Van

Cliburn. He too has large hands. Maybe some day, if you practice hard and diligently, you will also be able to write down some of the music that you hear, and play it for the enjoyment of others.

"This piano has sat sadly idle for probably as many years as Alfred King's piano has. If my brain can make my fingers work after so long a time, I will play for you a piece from Beethoven called Moonlight Sonata. Let's turn around and face the keys, black and white. It takes both colors to make music."

"Watch my hands," she said. She paused over the keys for a long time. Perhaps in doubt of her neglected talent. Perhaps saying a silent prayer. Perhaps thinking, getting in the mood.

Then her hands began moving over the keys rhythmically. Music came from the huge instrument as if by magic and filled the house. The boy listened in wonderment, awestruck by what he was hearing.

She finished. Silence. They sat for awhile, saying nothing. Finally Koro spoke softly. Reverently. "I can never quite understand this thing called religion. Alf and I talk much about it. I wish to say to you, Missus Leckner, that what you have played just now is closest to what I think religion must feel like."

Tears were in her eyes. She hugged him. "Thank you for the best compliment you could ever give me," she said quietly. "We will get along well together."

And so The-Boy-Who-Hears-Music began to play music that others could hear. Although still small, he had large hands, as Mrs. Leckner had pointed out, and learned to use them over the keys of the piano. He learned rapidly, as in all things. He loved making music come out of this large instrument and never resisted practicing. His teacher was delighted with her pupil. They were good for each other.

CHAPTER 17

It was a telephone call from the Skeen Elementary School to Mr. Alfred King.

"Mr. King, this is Ida Mason, principal here at the school. I would like to meet with you sometime regarding your Koro."

"Is the boy in trouble?"

"Oh no. Nothing like that. There is just a matter that I would like to discuss with you and get your opinion on. When would it be convenient for you to come to the school?"

"If it involves Koro, any time is convenient. How about tomorrow morning?"

"Nine o'clock?"

"Fine."

Alfred King removed his big western hat and knocked on the principal's door.

"Come in," said a pleasant female voice. She was tall, slim, dressed in a conservative baize business skirt, white blouse and matching blazer. She extended her hand and shook his firmly.

"I... I... am surprised to..." he stammered.

"To find that I am black?" she said, smiling.

"Quite frankly, yes, Miz Mason. As you know, there aren't too many in these parts. But I must add that aside from being surprised, I am very pleased."

"Please sit down. And to start off, you are Alfred and I am Ida," she said, smiling.

He slid his large frame into the chair facing her desk and slumped down comfortably, holding his hat in his lap. He liked this woman immediately.

"Yes, Alfred. I am black in a dominantly white, middle class community. I am a woman. I am single. I have a Ph.D., and have learned to speak English like the upper crust. And I am a school administrator. I have beat all of the odds."

"It is good that Koro will have someone to look out for him..."

"Although we are both black I cannot look out for him anymore than any of the other students," she cut him off solemnly. "He must learn to face what is in the world. As much as you would like to, you cannot protect him from what he must learn and face as he grows up. Do you not agree, Alfred?"

"Of course, Ida. You are absolutely right. It is just that..." His voice grew hoarse with emotion. "It is only because I love him so much. He is like my own grandson. I want what is best for him."

"I understand that you are a widely traveled man and that you have conquered more of your prejudices than most of us have, or you never would have brought the boy from Africa and adopted him."

She stood, took some change from her desk drawer and said, "What kind of pop do you want? We have a machine out in the hall."

"How about a root beer."

She brought him an ice cold root beer and herself a coke. "Now the purpose for which I called you, Alfred. I want to advance Koro a grade, skip to the next grade right now. What say?"

"You really think he is ready?"

"More than ready, Alfred—not just in his reading, writing, math, science, not just in subject matter—in his total thinking and reasoning. He is more advanced in his thinking regarding society and philosphical things. Surely you have noticed this."

"Yes. At times his maturity and wisdom frightens me."

"I dare say, Alfred, that in many areas the boy thinks much deeper than you or me. It is sometimes quite frightening."

"I thought that I was the only one aware of this. The boy and I have very adult conversations. I have never talked down to him. Yes, by all means, move him ahead if you think it best."

"Thank you, Alfred. It has been a real pleasure meeting you. Koro King couldn't be in better hands. He worships you," she said, standing and shaking his hand.

CHAPTER 18

"Think you're pretty smart nigger, don't you?" said Rolly Benson, pushing Koro. "Think you're a real smart nigger getting moved ahead a grade, huh?" He shoved him again.

"No, I don't think I am so smart," answered Koro. "I didn't ask to get advanced a grade. Teacher and principal thought that I should be in higher grade. And quit pushing me, Rolly."

"I'll push you all I want, nigger," Rolly said, getting angrier. He shoved the small black boy so hard that he fell down on the hard floor of the school hall. It was lunch time and the students were headed toward the lunch room.

"You no good, big mouthed bully," shouted Alice Goldtooth, coming up to them.

"Stay out of this, Injun," sneered Rolly.

Koro got up slowly from the floor. His eyes were wide with anger. His patience had run out. His fist shot out like a snake striking. It caught Rolly by surprise in the stomach. Whoosh! The air went out of him. His face turned red and he doubled over in pain, gasping for air.

"Hurray for you, Koro," shouted Alice. "I wondered how much more you could take from big mouth."

"I shouldn't have become so angry, Alice. It is not like me to do that," said Koro.

"You bet you shouldn't have done that, nigger," wheezed Rolly, as he began to get his breath back. "I'll get you. One of these days, I'll get you."

It became one of those weeks for Koro, when everything went wrong. He was thrown off his horse the next day after school while helping Richard Gonzalez round up some stray calves, and sprained his ankle and got bruised up a bit. Then he couldn't concentrate on his piano lesson and displeased Mrs. Leckner.

The final blow came on Friday when a sad letter came from Ole in Kenya. He said that the old Elder Monduli had died in his sleep. Monduli had been Koro's guardian for his young years, like a grandfather, father and brother. It made him feel a sadness that he hadn't yet felt in his young life.

Ole told him of unhappiness in many of the nations of Africa. People were starving in Ethiopia, Somalia and other nations. Wars were raging in South Africa and Rwanda. Much blood was being shed. Many refugees were fleeing into Tanzania and Kenya. Ole's letter ended:

> *My dear little friend, you have been blessed by going to America where you will have opportunities to become what you were meant to be. I believe that you have a special gift and a mission to fulfill. I think that the Giver is guiding you.*
> *Give Alfred King my love and regards.*
> *Your friend forever,*
> *Ole*

Old King saw the boys feelings. After supper he said, "Do you want to talk about how you feel, my boy?"

"Yes, Alf. Maybe we need to talk."

They sat by the big front window watching twilight come into the western sky and reflect upon the lake far out on the horizon.

After sitting quietly for awhile, enjoying the peacefulness of the evening, Koro said, "Alf, I have been praying every night before my sleep. I am trying to get what you call religion. My prayer every night is, 'Giver, give us love.' This is what I want most." He paused and then confessed, "I pray for love and yet I hit Rolly Benson hard in the stomach. I hit him in anger."

"Maybe he needed to be hit. Maybe it was good that you finally hit him."

"I don't think so, Alf. I think it will only make him hate me more. And I think of old Monduli going on into the unseen world. I don't think that he would want The-Boy-Who-Hears-Music to create hate."

"You are probably right, Koro. Hate only perpetuates more hate. And you don't need to try to get religion, my boy. Most religions dictate and indoctrinate what we should and shouldn't believe. I think that you have more religion right now than most people ever find in their entire lives. Your religion is one of humility and spirituality that is not based upon sets of rules, but comes from your heart. The best advice I can give you is to follow the music that you hear. I think that it will show you the path to follow. Be The-Boy-Who-Hears-Music, like you were in your village among your people."

PART III

GROWING UP

CHAPTER 19

Junior high school was in the same building, only in the larger half. It was different than the elementary though. There was a different teacher and room for each subject. Koro liked it. He liked learning and always had.

He had grown, grown, grown, in many ways. His body showed the outward growth which was phenomenal. He was now fifteen and over six feet tall. He had started shaving his head again and wearing the gold earrings of his Maasai heritage. He walked elegantly, quietly, proudly, taking on again, naturally, many of the ways of his people, though at the same time becoming more Americanized.

He had learned the game of basketball, loving it. He was a natural, excelling at it and playing center on his junior high team. Old King put up a hoop on the storage shed with plenty of cement. Each evening they all played a rough game. Big hulking Larry from Montana didn't pay much attention to the foul rule. He just bulled his way through, knocking everyone helter-skelter. Chuck of Colorado, being short and stocky became a long shot and free throw expert. Tall, skinny Dex was a dribble artist. Koro was a finesse player, knowing all of the smooth moves and shots of the game. Alfred and Gordo participated in the free throw contests. They were like a bunch of rowdy boys and they loved these friendly contests. Richard Gonzalez was the smallest, but fought the hardest, getting many elbows in the head. From all of this, Koro learned the give and take and competitiveness of the game.

Koro heard his music, still playing in his mind, coming from "out there somewhere," clearer, more distinctly, always guiding him. The music he played on Mrs. Leckner's and Alfred King's piano became more refined and beautiful. It was entrancing. His large hands moved over the keys like magic. He often entertained the cowhands in the evenings, with Mrs. Leckner as guest. He also had performed at school assemblies and at several churches that he and Alfred often visited.

It was on a moonless, rainy night that he was awakened by his music. It was loud and tempestuous like thunder and lightening rolling through the sky. The music drew him up and out of bed. He slipped silently into his clothes and walked trance-like down the hall and out the door. The music was pulling him, drawing him on through the fields like a mystical giant magnet, towards his piano teacher's house. Mrs. Leckner was in trouble. He knew it for certain.

When he reached her house he was drenched from the rain. He rang her doorbell and waited. No answer. He pounded on her door. No answer. He peered in through the window. A dim lamp burned on a small table by the couch. Then he saw her lying on the floor. He raised his foot and kicked open the door, rushing in and kneeling down beside her. She was lying on her side. He gently rolled her over and her eyes blinked open.

She smiled when she recognized him. "What took you so long, my boy?" she asked weakly. "Was your music playing too softly?"

He smiled back. "Where is your telephone?"

"On the kitchen wall by the table."

"Don't move," he commanded. "Stay right there."

He took a crocheted cover off the couch and put it over her and went to the phone. "Alf, this is Koro. I am at Mrs. Leckner's house. I found her on the floor. She is very sick and needs a doctor."

"Stay there with her," instructed Alfred King, not asking further questions. "I'll call for a medivac helicopter to take her to the University Medical Center in Salt Lake City. I'll send the boys over with two vehicles. Their headlights can direct the helicopter in."

"All right, Alf."

A small crowd of neighbors from nearby farms had gathered in the rain to watch, to help if needed, when the helicopter landed.

The little lady squeezed Koro's hand just before they lifted her stretcher into the helicopter. She whispered into his ear. "Thank you, my son. Keep my piano keys warm with your practices while I am away."

It was a stroke. Her right foot dragged. Her right hand became next to useless. She could smile with only the left side of her mouth, and her speech came with difficulty. Alfred King hired a live-in practical nurse for her when she returned home, a stout, buxom woman, whose happy personality filled the entire house.

"This is Agnes, Koro," Mrs. Leckner introduced them when he stopped by for his usual lesson. They hugged each other and were immediate friends, as though they had known each other for years.

"I am afraid my hands are useless to demonstrate anymore for you, Koro," she said wistfully. "But I have taught you about all that I can anyway. You have equaled, if not surpassed my playing. But promise me you will still come by and play for me at least once a week."

"I will surely do that, Mrs. Leckner."

"Would you play for Agnes and myself now. I want her to hear how you make the keys sing like a chorus of angels."

He seated himself and adjusted the piano seat just right. His long legs now easily reached the pedals. "This is one of my own bits of music I have made up," he said.

It was a concerto of melodious and mystical quality that could not be described, except as being completely original. It held the two women spellbound. When he finished they were silent for several seconds, their eyes misty.

"Thank you, my son," said the little gray haired woman who had taught him. "You are everything I hoped you would be. You play, not just mechanically, but from the heart. That is what makes a truly great musician."

CHAPTER 20

Since coming to America, Koro King had learned the word prejudice only too well. He had experienced it in its many forms, mostly
subtle, but often, openly hostile. Never, though, had he felt it so
hatefully aggressive as shown by his classmate Rolly Benson. Rolly
would elbow him as they passed in the school halls, trip him,
punch him, shove him, and hiss disgusting words at him con-
stantly. Outwardly, Koro accepted this passively, trying hard to
ignore it. Inwardly, he wondered why he was the object of such
bitter hatred.

It all exploded during the last week of junior high. The school
traditionally sponsored a 5-K cross country race, three-point-two-
miles, a grand event before school closed for summer vacation. The
winner would receive a gold plated trophy with his name and the
date to be later engraved upon it. Anyone could participate. Koro
was among the first to sign up. His tall, elegant frame had grown
to six-foot-four already. He loved to run, and his long legs were
natural for it. He was disappointed to find Rolly Benson suddenly
beside him at the starting line-up.

"Nigger, I'm going to show you how to run," said Rolly. "That
trophy will be mine. I won it last year and I'm a cinch for it again.
What makes you think you can run? You're a fairy, besides being a
coon. You wear earrings like a girl." He jerked one of Koro's gold
earrings, pulling his ear painfully.

Koro looked him coolly in the eyes. "In Africa, my people
walk or run everywhere. It was our only means of getting around.
I can run. I will show you how to run."

Rolly was taken off guard by the calm statement. "We'll see,"
he sputtered. "We'll see."

The starting gun sounded and fifty-six runners from all grades moved forward, legs churning. Rolly pushed Koro and tripped him at the same time, and he sprawled flat, his long arms and legs flaying. His knees and palms of his hands were scraped and bleeding. He pulled himself up and brushed his knees off, starting to run again with a slight limp. The whole pack of runners was now well ahead of him.

A ninth grader named David Sly took the lead and held it for the first mile and a half, with Rolly close behind. The rest of the pack gradually fell farther behind. Koro's legs adjusted and found their stride. He gained his second wind. He soon reached the pack and moved up into it, weaving in and out between other runners.

At two and one-half miles, Rolly took the lead. David Sly kept second place close behind Rolly. Koro had now passed the pack and a few competitors in between. He moved into third place, seeming to gain more speed with each long stride.

The finish line could be seen ahead. A crowd of students, faculty, farmers, ranchers and town people cheered wildly. Koro King passed David Sly and moved into second place. Rolly began to tire and slowed down considerably. Koro gained new speed and strength. He shot by Rolly easily, crossing the finish line a good twenty yards ahead of him.

People patted him on the back. "What a marvelous recovery," said Principal Ida Mason as she presented him the trophy. "A well deserved win, Koro."

Alf hugged him warmly. Rich, Dex, Chuck and Larry, his fellow cowboys, lifted him on their shoulders as they headed back toward the school.

Gordo yelled to him from back in the crowd. "Special dinner tonight for you, Koro."

His friend Alice met him back at the school and they walked into the building with their arms around each others waist. He had forgotten about Rolly, but suddenly he was confronted by him.

"You'll pay, nigger," he sneered. "It was all fixed between you and that nigger principal. Meet me after school at the ball field. I'll show you who is toughest and get even for that time you caught me off guard. You better be there or I'll let everyone know that you're yellow instead of black."

As Rolly stalked off, Alice said, "Don't go, Koro. He's not worth it. Everyone knows he's a bully."

"I have to, Alice. I must find out what's with this Rolly Benson. I've got to stop this hate he has somehow."

CHAPTER 21

The word had spread. Rolly had made sure of that, telling everyone how he was going to take care of that misfit nigger. A crowd had gathered at the ball field about a hundred yards west of the school. Rolly was dancing around in the center of those waiting for the action, shadow boxing and spewing out his usual bully talk.

"He'll never show. He won't dare come. His real color is yellow, not black."

"Oh yeah, Rolly," shouted someone in the crowd. "Wrong again. Here comes Koro now."

A cheer went out as they saw him in the distance. A frown of apprehension crossed Rolly's face. Perhaps he was remembering their earlier encounter years back when Koro had unexpectedly retaliated and punched him hard, knocking the wind out of him. He determined that it wouldn't happen again.

Koro walked quietly into the circle as the crowd parted for him. Some gave him words of encouragement and patted him on the back. He was still the hero and winner of the annual cross country race. No one liked Rolly Benson except a few of the so-called toughs of the school.

Rolly sneered at him. "Are you ready to fight, nigger? Old Rolly is ready to show you how it's done."

"It is not the way to solve differences," said Koro calmly.

"Well, it's my way. Put up your fists. Are you turning chicken already?" said Rolly, dancing around the tall, black boy, jabbing at the air.

"I am here, am I not? I didn't have to come."

"Looks like I get to tear you apart easy like," said Rolly, swinging at Koro's face.

Quickly the black boy moved his face back and Rolly's punch
went wide. Koro dodged the next two swings, but never put his
fists up in fighting stance. He never hit back.

The crowd was becoming excited, wanting some blood as most
spectator mobs do. "Hit him, Koro. Let him have it. Kill the bully.
Smash his big mouth," came shouts from the crowd.

Rolly's next swing hit Koro in the mouth. A groan came from
the crowd. Koro calmly wiped the blood from his mouth, but
would not raise his hands. His arms hung limply at his side. The
next punch hit him in the stomach and doubled him over. The
next one caught him to the side of his head near his right eye. It
immediately puffed up. Then another punch hit his jaw and
knocked him to the ground.

He pushed himself up to his knees and shook his head to clear
it.

"Had enough, yellow nigger?" taunted Rolly.

In answer to the question Koro King rose shakily to his feet
and stood defiantly, looking into the bully's eyes.

"Hit him, Koro. What's the matter? Teach him a lesson. Beat
him into the ground," came encouragement from the crowd.

Still he would not raise his arms to fight or even protect himself. Rolly swung his hardest and hit him in the nose. Blood spurted
out and he dropped again to the ground. With strained effort he
again got to his knees and was trying to stand, when out of the
crowd came a screaming figure like a wild animal. It was Alice
Goldtooth.

"It is enough. I'll kill you, Rolly Benson. I'll kill you," she
screamed, jumping on his back, clawing, scratching, hitting and
pulling his hair like an enraged beast.

Rolly let out a startled yell and finally manage to throw Alice
to the ground. "You damned squaw!" he shouted at her.

Sitting on the ground, she looked up at him with hate in her
eyes. "You'll pay for this, Rolly. I have a brother in Salt Lake City

who belongs to a gang called the Red Utes. They will teach you a lesson. You will pay, bully. You'll be sorry you ever did this."

"I'm not afraid of any wild Indians," he mumbled, as he hunched his shoulders and elbowed his way through the crowd.

"You'll pay, Rolly Benson. You'll be real sorry," Alice screamed after him.

She pushed herself up from the dirt and went to help Koro to his feet. The crowd dispersed, many shaking their heads and muttering, "Why wouldn't he fight? What's the matter with him?"

Alice took out a scarf and wiped the blood off his face. They walked off the field with their arms around each other's waist.

· · ·

Worse than the beating he took was the reception he received at home from his own cowboy brothers. Several students had already called the ranch to tell what had happened to Koro.

"Why wouldn't you fight him, Koro?" asked Chuck in bewilderment. "You are bigger than him. You could have beaten him good and he would never have bothered you again."

Old King was carefully washing the dried blood off his face from a basin, then applying antiseptic. Koro never even winched at the pain. His lip was split badly in two places. His nose was broken. His eye was swollen shut, but he seemed oblivious to it.

"Yeah," added Dex. "I can't understand why a big athletic guy like you wouldn't fight that bully and settle things once and for all. You're much tougher than him from riding and working hard here on the ranch. I know you could have whipped him good. I just can't understand why you didn't."

Larry, who was quiet by nature, remained silent, but looked at Koro strangely for a long while.

Hadn't his brothers heard of Ghandi, Martin Luther King, Jesus of Nazareth? Didn't they understand the message of these and other great ones? He had been reading their messages and he believed. Love was bette than hate. All peoples of earth should strive for understanding. Love of fellow beings brought peace. It was what the world needed. And yet the looks in his brother's eyes, and their statements, inferred that he was a coward for not fighting.

The white haired old man continued to doctor his black son's face. Finally he spoke. "My boy, whom I love dearly. Many times I have thought that I don't understand you very well. But now I think that I do. I think that at this moment I understand you more than I ever have before."

"And I think that I do too," added Rich Gonzalez quietly.

Koro, who had not shed a tear during his entire beating at the hands of Rolly Benson, now felt his eyes brimming over and flowing down his cheeks. Not saying a word in response to anyone, he walked slowly down the hall to his room.

CHAPTER 22

Rolly knocked the last pool ball into the side pocket. He hung up his que stick and collected his bets. He was good at pool. He ought to be; he played it regularly enough. Although he was under age, the manager let him play because he was good and attracted business. It was the only time anyone associated with him and they were mostly older pool bums.

He swaggered out on to the night streets of Skeen City. Most nights he thumbed a ride in and then bummed a ride home with some of the patrons. Tonight he felt especially good. He had beaten up that nigger Koro King and had cleaned up at the pool table. He would spend some of his seventeen dollars he had won on a huge steak smothered in onions and mushrooms.

As he started walking, Rolly saw the car pull up to the curb ahead of him. Several dark figures got out. The lights on the marquee of the movie theater shone on their shoulder length black hair. They wore red bands tied around their heads. He sensed trouble and turned to head the other way. Two more of the shadowy figures were walking toward him from that direction. From both sides they were closing in on him. He felt trapped. Panic bubbled up inside him. He started running and turned into the alley by the pool hall. He could outrun them and escape in the dark. But he ran into a dead end. The alley was blocked by another building at its end.

He turned and saw the shadowy figures moving into the alley. Suddenly he realized that this was Alice Goldtooth's brother and his gang of Red Utes. Why had he doubted and sluffed off her words as an idle angry threat? His panic turned to terror.

They had him cornered. "Are you Rolly Benson?" asked the

first one to reach him.

"What's it to you?" he replied.

"It's him all right," said the Ute.

A fist slammed into his stomach. He gasped for breath as another fist caught him in the face. He slumped to the ground. He vaguely could feel them lift him up. Two of them held him while blows hit him again and again and again. He saw flashes of bright orange... and then nothing.

...

Koro awoke suddenly and sat up in bed. His music was playing wildly, a tempestuous symphony, pulling, pulling him out of bed. He groaned as the pain of his injuries hit him. But he struggled into his jeans and boots painfully. He buttoned his shirt as he padded down the hall and out to the bunkhouse.

He shook Richard Gonzalez gently. "Rich... Rich, I hate to wake you up, but someone needs our help in Skeen City. Could you drive me in?"

"Huh? What? Oh, Koro, what is it?"

"Someone needs help... in Skeen. Could you drive us in there?"

Richard never questioned. "Sure. I'll get the jeep and meet you in front of the ranch house."

They drove in silence until Richard asked, "Are your cuts and bruises pretty sore?"

"Not really. Not that bad. My mouth and nose are kind of throbbing. I'll be okay though."

They reached Skeen. It was well past midnight. Most establishments had closed. Skeen, being a small country town, didn't have much night life. Most people farmed or ranched. Worked hard. Most folks went to bed with the sun and beat it up the next morning. The lights on the pool hall sign and the movie theater were all that were on, and a couple of dim market and business signs.

"Where to, Koro?" asked Richard.

"Just cruise up and down main street pretty slow."

They were on their third sweep. "Over there, Rich. In that alley. Looks like someone on the ground."

"Where? I don't see anything."

"Back up to that alley, between the movie theater and the pool hall. There! See. Lying there on the ground. A body."

Koro jumped out and ran into the alley. He knelt by what looked like a pile of rags. Richard parked the jeep at the curb and followed him. Koro knelt by the bundle and rolled it over. It gave a faint moan.

"It's Rolly, Rich. Rolly Benson. He looks in bad shape."

"Is that the same guy that worked you over?"

"Yeah. That's him. Rolly Benson."

"Kind of ironic, huh. You helping a guy that hates you."

"We need to get him to a doctor, Rich. He looks pretty bad."

Koro started to lift his head up and he opened his eyes and groaned. Then he recognized his rescuer and his eyes flipped open wide. "You! Get away!" he mumbled softly. "Leave me alone. I don't need any help from you."

"You need help from anyone you can get it from. You are in pretty bad shape, Rolly."

"It was Alice's wild Indians. A bunch of damned wild Indians," he managed in a bare whisper. "Some friend you got there."

His head rolled back and he slipped into unconsciousness again.

"Rich, can you give me a hand? Let's get him into the jeep. We can take him to that all night clinic at the end of town. He needs a doctor."

CHAPTER 23

It was nearing two a.m. as they drove out of the quiet, sleeping town of Skeen. The doctor determined that Rolly had broken ribs, broken jaw and nose, and a hand that looked like it had been smashed with a club or brick or something similar. Further x-rays and exams would be needed to determine the full extent of his injuries. The doctor had taken all of the information, called the police and said he would contact Rolly's home.

When they were on the darkened highway back to the ranch, Richard looked in amazement at Koro and asked quietly, "Koro, can you tell me more about your music, this music that you hear, that kind of guides you, tells you of things... well, things like tonight."

Koro was silent for a long time and Richard thought he wouldn't answer such a personal question. "Promise that you won't belittle, that you will accept," said Koro finally. "I mean that you will accept what I tell you as the way I know it to be. You don't have to believe it in your way of thinking. You don't even have to understand. Just accept it as my truth. Okay?"

"I promise."

"To your way of thinking, my music might best be compared to one's conscience, a guardian angel guiding you, or the still small voice speaking to you. But my music is more clear, more real, much more than that. I truly believe it was a gift given to me for some reason. It all began with my birth. I remember being born..."

"You mean that you actually remember your own birth?" asked Richard incredulously.

"Yes. This is how I remember it: myself, the seed that will become me, is germinating in the soil, the water and elements within my mother's womb. What a marvelous and miraculous garden. As her stomach swells, I am also growing and developing. I am all the time aware of myself. I am becoming more of the ME that I will be in this new world I am going to. I am now embryo. Soon I will be fetus. In nine months the miracle is completed. The fruit of the womb is ripe.

"I am pushing and struggling to get out. I am breaking the dam holding back the water. I am swimming, swimming, and finally my head breaks to the surface. Hands help me out into the air. I am born into this new life. My eternal spirit now inhabits my mortal body. I am now the ME of this world, earth.

"I am breathing air and I see earth light for the first time, as though through a glass darkly. The root attaching me to my mother is severed. I am quickened. I am an independent human being, though totally dependent on others in my new state of being. I am mortal. I am the new ME arrived in my second home, Earth. I am ready to begin my new adventures. Alone, but not alone. I hear music that has arrived with me. The music is beautiful beyond description. Enlightening, uplifting beyond all explanation. Most people are born between veils or curtains, not having the power to remember the before birth nor to see the beyond after death. I have been given a gift: my music. I can remember it all.

"I remember being held by a circle of hands. There is a circle formed by six men. They are the *Ilpayiani*, the Elders of my tribe. They are gently moving me up and down in a motion like the waves of the ocean so that I will be charmed and not cry. I cry anyway, but it is *enkiseer*, cries of happiness. One of the men is talking. Their eyes are all closed. As he talks on, the waves get bigger as I am bounced up and down. One of the men opens an eye and peaks at me. Our eyes lock together. We understand each other and I laugh out loud. He is Monduli, the one who becomes my godfather. That was before glaucoma took his sight away.

"The man talking is praying to *Engai*, the Supreme God of Heaven. He asks *Engai* to bless me with special abilities and with strength to accomplish many things while on earth. But I know that *Engai* has already given me a special gift: my music which will guide me through my earth journey.

"The waves stop. The talking stops. The men open their eyes. They all chant my name which they have chosen. Later when they learned of my gift, they shorten my name to Koro, which means old man in another language. They make me a *Laibon*. It is a title of honor. Later, when I have found language, I tell Monduli of my gift of music. It is then that my people begin to call me The-Boy-Who-Hears-Music. And I become one who is highly honored, being just a child.

"And that is how it was and is, Rich. I remember it all."

Richard Gonzalez was awe struck. He whispered quietly, "Incredible. Absolutely marvelous!"

CHAPTER 24

Koro awoke and groaned. He was stiff and sore. His lips were swollen. One eye was puffed shut. A deep cut marked his cheek. But all he could think about was how much more Rolly Benson must be hurting.

When he got on the school bus no one spoke to him. Everyone looked away. Alice Goldtooth was not on the bus. He felt alone. Sad.

During third period class Principal Ida Mason sent for him. He wondered what she wanted, as he knocked shyly on her open door. She smiled as she looked up from her desk. "Come in, Koro. Please sit down."

He eased his long body into the chair facing her desk. On the wall behind her were framed pictures of all of the presidents of the United States. On one side wall was an autographed picture of Mohamud Ali in his famous boxing pose. On the other side wall was an autographed picture of Martin Luther King. She observed him as he noticed the pictures.

"Yes, I met both of those gentlemen long ago," she said. "They are not necessarily my heroes, however. I am cautious about having heroes. They often have clay feet and let us down, especially when we find that they are human and have weaknesses like the rest of us."

She pushed her chair away from her desk and leaned back. "I keep these pictures there because they remind me that there might be a time for peace and there might be a time to fight." Then Ida Mason looked straight into his eyes. "You look like you've been through a hay bailer. Why wouldn't you fight Rolly Benson? Why did you just stand and let him beat you so mercilessly? I saw him trip you at the race. I know how he has bullied you ever since you came here."

He looked surprised.

"Oh, I know all about the fight. Those things can't be kept secret in a school," she continued. "I have already heard at least a dozen versions of the incident. Many students think you were a coward, afraid of Rolly. I don't believe that. Can you tell me why you wouldn't fight back."

His head went down. He stared at the floor.

"If you don't wish to discuss it, that's fine. I won't force the issue."

Slowly he raised his head and looked into her eyes again. "Miz Mason, I did not fight Rolly because it would have made him hate me more. I do not wish to have more of his hatred. I do not understand his hatred, but I do not wish to add to it."

They looked into each others eyes for several moments.

"You are a difficult boy to understand, Koro, but I am learning to understand you more each day and each year since you first came here as a small child. Now you tower above everyone in the school. I think that you made the right choice in not fighting. It took much more courage on your part. I am very proud of you."

He managed a weak smile, then winced at the pain in his cracked lips.

"Would you like to know something about Rolly Benson? It is my idea of why he treats you as he does."

"Yes, I certainly would like to know what Rolly has against me, Miz Mason. I never could figure him out. I tried to be his friend."

She tapped her pencil on her desk and thought how much she should reveal. "Rolly lives alone with his father. His mother and two younger sisters left several years ago because the father abused them. He drinks a lot and beats Rolly. Rolly's hate builds up inside of him. He probably releases it by being a bully. He picked you as his particular scapegoat. Our social worker has visited the home many times, but there hasn't been sufficient evidence for the court to step in."

"I didn't know this. I didn't have any idea, Miz Mason."

"Knowing doesn't make it easier on you. And it makes me even more proud of you for helping Rolly when he was hurt."

He looked surprised again.

"Oh, yes. I know that too. I received a call from the Health Clinic. Rolly's condition is quite serious. They had to move him to the Medical Center in Salt Lake City. I have pieced most of it together. And I know that it was Alice Goldtooth who got her brother and his gang to do this terrible deed.

"We are preparing a referral to the juvenile court regarding Rolly and his father." She paused and looked at him seriously. "And I am going to phone the authorities at the Ute Reservation requesting them not to allow Alice to return next year..."

"Oh no!" he interrupted. "You can't do that, Miz Mason. I mean... please don't do that. It would kill Alice. She is a smart girl and wants an education. Please, you must allow her to return next year. What she did was wrong. But she did it for me. She is my best friend. She was the first one to make me feel welcome when I came here. Please let her come next school year. We will be going into the high school and she has looked forward to that."

"Well... I will have to think about that. I will at least think over what you have said. You may go now. And, Koro, have a good summer and tell Alfred King hello for me."

CHAPTER 25

Alfred King was getting old. Real old. He couldn't deny it any longer. He had to admit it to himself. The realization took hold when he had to have help mounting his horse, or had to mount from a fence rail. He knew that his days of earth life were numbered. So one day in July he announced to his cowhands after another scrumptious supper prepared by Gordo, "We have been working too hard. Let's have a few days of fun and go rodeoing."

They all cheered and threw their hats in the air.

Rodeos are a big thing in Utah, and are held in almost every community down to the smallest. They are held during the week of July 24th to help celebrate that day in 1847 when the Mormon pioneers under the leadership of Brigham Young, entered the Salt Lake Valley.

Brigham, from his sick bed in a wagon, pushed himself to a sitting position, surveyed the valley below him from the mouth of Immigration Canyon, and announced to his weary followers that this was the place. This would be where they would build up their City of Zion. This was where they would finally worship God in peace after their years of persecution at the hands of vicious mobs.

"But it is only a desert. A barren wasteland of sagebrush and alkali land and a salty lake," cried his followers.

"Then we will make the desert blossom like a rose," replied Brigham Young.

Now, many years later, his prophecy has been fulfilled through pain, suffering, determination and just plain hard work. Brigham Young was a hero to Alfred King, although he himself was not a Mormon. He often told his cowhands that any man that could lead his downtrodden, driven Saints over hundreds of miles of dust, mud, cold, snow and swollen rivers, all the while, fighting snakes, hunger, thirst, Indians, sickness and burying many along the way, had to be a strong man. A humble man. A man of faith. A man of God.

So the 24th of July celebrated that occasion, perhaps a bigger celebration even than the 4th of July. Besides rodeos, there were parades, chuck wagon breakfasts in parks, square dancing in the streets, and of course, religious services in all of the Mormon chapels throughout Utah.

"Let's go to the rodeo in Ogden," continued Old King. "I think it's a better one than Salt Lake City's." He added, "And I expect you to participate, not just sit and watch the events. You fellows are as fine a cowboys as any others I have seen. So sign up and get in there and compete. Of course Gordo and I have earned our rest so we will watch from the announcer's booth where we will be served excellent refreshments accorded to our highly earned status."

They all laughed.

...

They pulled two horse trailers, one small one and one large one, and took three vehicles. Dex would need his own horse for the bulldogging or steer wrestling. Larry was going to be a pick-up man, which required that horse and rider work together as one. The pick-up man was a risky job requiring that he and his horse move in rapidly to take a rider safely off a bucking bronco or bull onto their own horse as soon as the horn sounded the end of their ride.

Richard chose bareback bull riding where the rider rode a bucking brahma bull with similar rules to the bronco riding.

Koro had entered the bareback bucking bronco contest. He felt that he would not completely be an American cowboy until he had ridden a bucking bronco in a rodeo. He had helped break several horses at the ranch, but had never ridden a bronco alone in a competition. He was quiet all during the ride to the Ogden rodeo grounds.

"Nervous, Koro?" asked Alfred, as they arrived at the stadium.

"More than nervous, Alf. I'm plain scared," replied Koro.

The old man chuckled. "I don't blame you. I'm glad it's you and not me going to mount that bronco. But you aren't alone in your feelings. I dare say that every cowboy participating will have butterflies in his guts. Once that critter comes out of the chute, all you will think about is staying on his back for ten seconds that will seem like ten years. And remember, Koro, hang tight to the rope with only one hand. Let your other hand flap free and help balance you on the horses. Balance, that's the secret. Clamp your legs in tight when you can also. "Then the old man smiled. "And remember to have fun."

They did have fun, being with other cowboys, being wild. Free. Smelling the leather, horse sweat, manure and straw. Feeling equal to every other cowboy. Feeling a part of the excitement.

After the rodeo, late at night, they lined up to get their thirty-two ounce steaks, beans and sourdough bread at the park adjacent to the rodeo grounds and the stadium. They ate, talked and mingled with other cowboys, some from as far away as Nebraska, Kansas, Oklahoma, the Dakotas and even Canada. Koro had never been so happy and excited.

"I did it, didn't I?" Koro kept asking. "I stayed on him for the full ride."

"You sure did," assured Larry. "I was the one that took you off at the horn. You rode it out for the full ten count."

"That makes me a real American cowboy now, doesn't it?"

"You've been a cowboy for years, Koro," said Gordo. "You've done everything with your brother at the ranch."

"But now I have been on a bucking bronco. I will remember this day for all of my life."

Chuck, with his shoulders and chest as strong as a bull, had been the only one of them to score in the money. He had entered both the calf roping and the steer wrestling. He had taken second

place in the bulldogging contest where the rider races out after the
steer, slips off his horse, grabs the critter by his horns, digs in his
heels to stop their forward motion, and twists the steers neck until
he flops flat on his side.

"You would be a champion among my Maasai people, Chuck,"
said Koro. "You could win easily in our *Embolata Olkiteng*."

"What's that?" asked Chuck, stuffing another bite of choice
steak into his mouth.

"It could be where your American saying, 'Taking the bull by
the horns' came from. It is a contest my people have of holding the
bull by the horns and wrestling it to the ground. Only we don't
use horses and the bull is a brahma bull like the ones you ride here
in the bucking bull contest."

"No thanks," said Chuck. "I'll stick to our game. Those
brahma's look too mean to me. Rich can ride those critters, and
Dex too, all they want. Not for me."

They all laughed happily, a good feeling of comradery.

CHAPTER 26

Next to cowboying and perhaps even more than cowboying, Koro King liked learning. His hunger and thirst for learning never ceased. His curiosity was boundless, his eagerness and enthusiasm were like a boiling pot bubbling over. So he was happy that school was starting again.

The bus would take him and his fellow students into the high school in Ogden City, fifteen miles to the south. Skeen Junior High and other junior highs in other small surrounding communities fed into the Ben Franklin High School in Ogden, making its student body near eighteen hundred students.

He was happy to be on the noisy school bus again. He was even happier when at the next stop a familiar voice shouted as she got on, "Hey, Koro, how you doing? Can I sit by you?"

Just like old times. His faithful friend, Alice Goldtooth. He was so glad to see she had come back. She plunked down beside him. "I really messed things up good, huh. I mean bringing in my brother and his gang. I got to thank you for putting in a good word for me, helping to get me okayed to come back. Miz Mason told me."

"Forget it, Alice," he said, smiling.

"Man, you're still growing like a tall weed in a manure pile," Alice commented, looking him over. "I'll have to stand on a box to talk to you."

He laughed. "My brothers at the ranch measured me and said I'm about six-foot-six-and-a-half. They keep yelling 'Duck!' or watch your head whenever I'm inside a building. Guess I'll go out for the basketball team at high school. They are after me to play. Besides being tall, I'm used to being pushed around when I play with the rough neck cowboys at the ranch. They don't believe in rules."

At the next stop all talking suddenly ceased. There stood Rolly Benson by the road. He motioned to the driver, who turned off the engine and stepped down out of the bus. In a few seconds he got back on, turned to the students on the bus. "Koro King, Rolly Benson wants to talk with you. Five minutes, okay?"

The bus became deathly quiet. Koro stood and walked down the aisle, wondering what to expect. No one had seen Rolly since he beat Koro mercilessly last spring, although they had all heard of his beating by the Red Utes. Faces pressed against the windows as Koro stepped out of the bus.

"Hello, Rolly. How you doing?" he asked, his mind racing with anxiety and curiosity.

"I'm not going back to school. Not going into the high school, at least not here," he said, staring at the ground.

Koro said nothing, wondering why he wasn't returning to school.

"I'm going to North Carolina," continued Rolly, still talking to the ground. "Going there to live with my uncle and aunt." He looked up for the first time and gave a weak half smile. "Maybe they can rehabilitate me."

Rolly looked thinner, cleaner. He took his hands out of his pockets and struggled for words. "I... I apologize... I am sorry..." He choked back emotions. "I am sorry for how I treated you all that time... I... will you shake my hand?"

Koro stuck out his big hand and they shook hands. Koro now towered in height above Rolly. All of the faces pressed against the bus windows were awe struck.

"And I want to thank you for helping me even after what I did to you," Rolly added. He put his hands back in his pockets, hunched his shoulders, and turned to walk away. Then he stopped and turned around again. "Oh, and tell Alice it's okay. She's a good friend to you. I deserved what I got."

No one uttered a sound as Koro got back on the bus and took his seat. They had just witnessed a miracle.

CHAPTER 27

The Maasai boy from Kenya, The-Boy-Who-Hears-Music, Koro King, became very popular in high school. He made center on the varsity basketball team his sophomore year. He was selected to the All-State team his junior year. By senior year his height had sky-rocketed to six-feet-nine-inches tall. Scouts from many universities had their eyes on him. His grade point average was 3.98. He gave a sold-out piano concert to raise funds for the school band. He was what could be called an all-around student. He was a friend to everyone. That is, he was a friend to everyone until he crossed a certain invisible line, a line that still couldn't be easily crossed if the color of your skin was black.

Alice Goldtooth had nominated Koro for student body president and had become his campaign manager. Students who had seemed to be his friends suddenly became wary and aloof. Placards appeared from the opposition:

PLAY BASKETBALL
PLAY MUSIC-
BUT DON'T PLAY POLITICS

* * * *

BLACKS AREN'T LEADERS!

* * * *

NO NIGGER PRESIDENT

* * * *

The green-eyed monster of suspicion, bigotry and hate had again looked upon him, more fiercely than ever before. He was hurt inside. Really hurt... deep down inside.

He asked himself: "Who are friends? What are friends? Are they just friends when you do what they want?... Do what they want you to think?... What they want you to do?... Want you to be?... Aren't there friends who just like Koro King the way he is? The way God made him?"

At supper that evening he was quiet... didn't enter into the banter... didn't enter into the singing after, as Gordo played his guitar. He couldn't fake his feelings.

"Come on out on the porch and sit with me a spell," said old King, after everyone split up.

He poured them both a tall, cold glass of orange juice and they carried it out to the south end of the porch, which extended the full length of the ranch house. There was a big outdoor couch which they plunked down on. The view was unobstructed in that particular spot clear out to the Great Salt Lake. A full moon lit up the world, making long shadows almost like day. It formed its silver highway stretching across the simmering lake.

They drank in silence until Alfred King said, "Care to talk about it, to tell me what's bothering you, my son?"

The moonlight glistened off the wetness on Koro's cheeks. "I thought they were my friends, Alf. I thought they were all my friends," he said, choking back his emotion. "It's that word I have learned so well... prejudice. I think it has left me alone and it pops up again to torment me...

"You know that Alice has run me for student body president. Well the hate signs have come out against me. People I thought were my friends aren't friendly anymore. This... this thing about me being black. It is dividing the school... breaking it apart."

"Want me to have a chat with the principal?"

"Thanks, Alf, but no. You can't force people to change their opinions. You can't force their thoughts and make them think differently. Those things take a long time, I guess."

He stifled a sob and old King blew his own nose into his large red handkerchief.

"Opinion can change, my boy. Thoughts and minds can be changed. But you are right, it takes a long time. Sometimes generations. "He gathered his thoughts and went on. "Remember when you were just a little guy, when I first brought you here. I tried many times to tell you, to prepare you for what you would have to face. What you would be up against. But you were so innocent, so full of happiness. Full of enthusiasm about being in this great free country of America, that you couldn't or wouldn't in your wildest imaginings, foresee that there were many people of little tolerance for anyone or anything... different. Differences seem to bring out hate in some folks. But it is really fear. Fear of something that they don't know about or don't even want to learn about or understand. But, Koro, I still think that those kinds are in the minority. I still think that most folks are fair and kind and considerate. Look at your miracle with Rolly Benson. Change can happen in the worst of us."

They were quiet again, as the shadows lengthened and changed like listening forms of dark spirits. The moon moved closer toward the western horizon of the lake.

"I never told you, my boy, but I even appealed to your junior high principal, Ida Mason," Alfred continued. "I thought, her skin color being the same as yours, that I might hint to her to maybe protect you, look out for you, you know, put some kind of plastic bubble around you to keep this hurt, this prejudice thing away from you.

"But she, having experienced it throughout her life, was wiser than me. She told me that you would have to learn to handle it in your own way. Remember, Koro, that she was able to become a black principal in a white community. And I am still amazed at your miracle with Rolly Benson. Perhaps you can make other

miracles happen. Just hang in there through the bad times. There
will be the good ones, too."

Koro wiped his eyes with the back of his hand. "Thanks, Alf.
Thanks for reading my thoughts and moods. Thanks for your support and always being here when I need you. I'll just let things
take their course for now."

CHAPTER 28

"Please be seated, Koro," said Principal Oscar Wright. He peered over round, silver rimmed spectacles on the end of his thin, hooked nose. His bald head reflected sunlight from the single office window that looked out toward the baseball diamond. His small, wiry body seemed out of place in the huge black swivel chair, as it hunched over the even larger walnut desk.

Koro eased his tall frame into the chair facing the principal's desk. He had never been this close to the man before. He was so tiny. He reminded Koro of a frightened mouse. Koro's eyes swept around the office: a metal file cabinet in the far corner, behind the desk, three chairs, besides the one he sat in. To the side opposite the window, a bookcase filled with educational books. On the walls hung many framed diplomas, degrees and certificates. A portrait of George Washington hung high on the wall behind the desk. On the desk were three baskets labeled: In, Out, Pending. A bronze bust of John F. Kennedy sat on one corner of the desk.

"My, but you are growing taller each time I see you," Principal Wright was saying. "How tall are you, my boy?"

"I think I'll reach six-ten by basketball season, Sir."

"And hopefully you will take us to a state championship."

"Our team has a very good chance this year, Mr. Wright."

Principal Wright coughed nervously and adjusted his glasses. "Koro, a rather delicate situation has come up, a rather touchy matter indeed. I am sure you have seen some of the nasty placards that have appeared in the halls and around the campus referring to yourself."

"Yes, Sir."

"It grieves me to see this sort of thing happening at our school in this day and age. I didn't think this kind of bigotry was still with us. But it is here. The sad thing is that it is splitting our school in two, dividing our student body."

"Elections always divide people," cut in Koro. "It is my understanding that the purpose of elections is to have two or more factions, and the candidate with the most votes is the winner."

"Yes, yes of course. But things are getting mean, out of control, worse each day. I have given much consideration to the matter, and I feel that it would be for the best good of the school if... if you would remove your name from the ballot... withdraw from the campaign. It would calm things down and return our old school spirit. Could you do this, my boy? Could you make this sacrifice for the sake of the school?"

Silence in the room. Only sounds of PE classes out on the athletic field.

Koro pulled himself up straight in the chair and looked into the principal's eyes, who quickly looked away. "Mr. Wright, I have never been a quitter and I don't intend to quit now just because things are getting mean. If my name is to be removed from the election campaign you will have to remove it. May I leave now?"

"Yes, of course. But please consider what I have requested."

...

The next day Alice Goldtooth was called into the principal's office.

"You are Koro King's campaign manager, the one who nominated him for student body president, are you not?"

"Yes, Mr. Wright. I think Koro would make a fine student body president. I have known him for many years. He is a person of outstanding qualities."

"I am aware of that, Alice. But you also see what is happening to our student body. It is being torn apart by this racial thing.

"So?"

"So I think that you had better withdraw Koro as a candidate..."

"I think that would be a very chicken thing to do," Alice inter-rupted.

"You are out of line, Alice."

"You bet I am out of line. I wouldn't want to be in line with those few creeps who are a bunch of red neck bigots. I thought this civil rights thing had been resolved years ago. And isn't this a student election?"

"Yes, of course it is a student election, but you can't legislate people's opinions and prejudices."

"If it is a student election then why is the administration inter-fering?" Alice's eyes were flashing anger. "And you are the administration, Mr. Wright."

"It is only because things are getting out of hand, Alice. And it is my job to keep them under control. And I am asking you, as Koro King's campaign manager, to withdraw his name as a candidate."

"Well, I am telling you quite plainly, Mr. Wright, that I will not remove his name as a candidate. This is still America, and Ben Franklin High is part of America. And if you remove his name as a candidate, then I say you are a damned chicken."

Alice Goldtooth was suspended from school for a week. Koro King's posters were taken down and his name removed from the ballots.

CHAPTER 29

It had not been a good year for Benjamin Franklin High School Principal Oscar Wright, despite the fact that the basketball team had taken the state championship, led by their All-American high school candidate center, Koro King. Graduation time was approaching and that same Koro King turned up as valedictorian with a three-point-nine-seven grade point average, translating to number one ranked student in his graduating class.

Prejudice again raised its evil head: a few phone calls and anonymous letters from parents objecting to the only black in the school being given such an honor. And, of course, the few radical trouble-making students again protesting. The pressure began building up again and the hand-wringing anxiety began flooding Oscar Wright's mind. What should he do? A telephone call ended the dilemma and made his decision for him.

"Principal Wright speaking," he snapped into the phone.

"Hello, Oscar. This is Ida Mason at Skeen Junior High."

"Ah, yes, Miss Mason..."

"Ida, just Ida, Oscar."

"Yes, Ida. What can I do for you?"

"One of your students, Koro King, has been on my mind. He was one of our finest students when he was here at Skeen Junior High. A brilliant boy, high ethical standards, great citizenship. I hear that he has achieved top ranking in your graduating class and is to be valedictorian."

"Well... er... yes... he has achieved number one ranking. We are considering him as valedictorian, considering ratifying him that is."

"What do you mean, considering him? A valedictorian earns

that right, achieves it by ranking number one scholastically in his class."

"Yes, but there are extenuating circumstances, Miss Mason..."

"Ida."

"Yes, Ida, there are some things that have cropped up that bring about other considerations."

"Look, Oscar. Cut out the crap. I heard about that fiasco you called a student election. The way you handled that was a downright chicken thing."

Silence. Oscar was beginning to sweat and pulled at his collar. He laughed nervously into the phone. "You are the second one to have called me chicken this year regarding that."

"It is true. You were chicken. That was absolutely disgusting the way you squelched a student election because of a little pressure from a few rabble-rousers. But a valedictorian is different, Oscar. It is earned. It is cut and dried. I hope you are not planning to override that well known fact."

"I have to do what I think is best for the school," he replied, his voice beginning to squawk weakly.

"Once, I promised myself that I would not interfere nor try to protect this boy because his skin color happened to be the same as mine," continued Ida Mason calmly. "But now I am going to break that promise. If you try to take away that young man's earned right as valedictorian you will feel pressure like you have never felt it before. I will put you on a very hot seat, Oscar."

"Are you threatening me?" His voice squeaked two octaves higher.

"Yes!"

Silence and heavy breathing into the phone.

"Oscar, are you still there?" she asked. "Are you listening to what I say?"

"Yes. I'm listening."

"I have never used my influence before. But if you deny Koro King this right, I will crush you, Oscar. I know influential people on the State Board of Education, and in the governor's office. With

a couple of phone calls I can make this a national incident overnight. It will ruin you, Oscar. Do you understand what I am saying to you?"

"Yes, Miss Mason. I understand."

"It's Ida, Oscar. Just plain Ida," she said, as she hung up the
phone.

CHAPTER 30

There had been a prayer. The superintendent had spoken. The school madrigals sang. Then Koro King walked to the podium and adjusted the microphone up as high as it would go. He was humble. He was distinguished in his cap and gown. He was elegant. The school auditorium was filled to capacity. Many were standing at the back.

"Superintendent. Principal Wright. Faculty. Fellow students," he began. He paused and looked out over the audience. "No one stands here in my position alone. I am here because of the help and support of many individuals. I would commit a sin of ingratitude if I did not acknowledge them.

"First I thank the Great God, the Heavenly Father of us all. The native people of Kenya called Him *Engai*. My own Maasai people called Him *Natero Kop*. He is the Giver of all things. Next I thank my parents, although I never knew them, for they brought me here to earth. In their place was my Godfather, Monduli, an old, blind Elder of our tribe who taught me what is right and what is wrong. He told me that I was someone special and to always strive for excellence. I also thank my elder brother and mentor, Ole, who tutored me on the path I should follow. He taught me your language called English, and also two other languages besides my native Maasai tongue."

He paused again and looked over the audience, smiling at his "family" in the front row.

"I now wish to thank those from this country who helped make me an American. My cowboy brothers at the ranch: Gordo, Richard, Larry, Chuck and Dex. They have been like blood brothers, family to me.

"Much thanks to my dear Mrs. Leckner who taught me to play my music for the enjoyment of others.

"It is very hard for a six-foot-ten person, whose skin color is black, to find true friends among strangers in a mostly white community. I have had wonderful team mates, classmates and many acquaintances. But true friends are scarce at best. I acknowledge such a true friend named Alice.

"I appreciate the support and faith placed in me by my junior high principal, Miss Ida Mason." He smiled openly at her.

"Now, last and foremost, I acknowledge my love for the man who has been father, grandfather, brother and friend to me, the man who took me off a dusty trail in Kenya, brought me here and made me into my dream, an American cowboy."

The audience laughed hardily.

"This man loved me, a lonely, dirty, ragged, little Maasai orphan. He brought me here to America, my far off dream. He gave me faith in myself and pride. Please stand, beloved father, Alfred King."

The white haired old man arose from his seat with effort and waved his white cowboy hat to acknowledge the wild cheering, while Koro King smiled proudly.

When the cheering subsided, he became serious. "If there is a theme to my remarks tonight, let it be called differences. I wish for each of us this night to ponder upon differences. To acknowledge the differences in each other and in ourselves. Each of us is different from everyone else. No one has the same set of fingerprints of anyone else in the world. Each of us is unique in some way. There are tall, short, skinny, fat, shy, boisterous. Different eyes. Different hair. Different skin: white, tan, brown, black, red, yellow."

He paused. The audience was very quiet. "And isn't it wonderful that there are these differences? Wouldn't it be boring if we were all the same? And who would decide who we would be the same as?

"Now by acknowledging differences, can we learn tolerance of these differences? I have met with intolerance in this very school, as most of you know. Why? Because by fate I was born in Africa with a black skin."

Many faces in the audience looked down at the floor and fidgeted nervously. There was not a sound in the auditorium.

"Think upon the great ones we have all learned about in our studies," he continued. "The philosophers, the scientists, the inventors, the medical people, the reformers of every country and society.

"If Edison had been a conformist and thought like everyone else, would we have had the electric light and dozens of these inventions of convenience? If the Wright brothers had listened to the scoffers and critiques, would we have had modern jet air travel? And what of the printed word which Gutenberg started? And what of the American founding fathers, the ones who came up with the Declaration of Independence and the Constitution? And what of the discoverers of preventive vaccines, inoculations and vaccinations? And the steamboat, and the cotton gin... and on and one and on... were those individuals like everyone else?... Did they think and act like everyone else?

"Differences. How wonderful."

Everyone's attention was centered on the tall, imposing, black valedictorian. The one reminding them of what they should know too well, putting many of them to silent shame.

"Many of you may know that I have been offered several full ride basketball scholarships, complete expenses paid, to some of the most prestigious basketball universities in America. I am turning them all down."

A gasp arose from the audience.

"Yes, you heard correctly. I am turning them down and I will tell you why. First, let me say that they are not true scholarships. Scholarships infer scholastic excellence based upon academic achievement and high test scores. Not one of these universities has asked about my academic record. If I don't meet their standards they assure me that they will help me to meet these requirements. No, my fellow students, they don't really care about my academics. They want to buy me so that I can put a ball through a hoop for their basketball team.

"Make no mistake. I love the game. I love basketball. But it seems that if you were born with genes that push you to near seven feet tall, and have reasonable coordination to put the ball through the hoop several times each game, you can name your college and later your price in the NBA.

"Or if you happen to be born with a strong body that grows to two-hundred-eighty pounds of solid muscle, and you learn to run the hundred in so many seconds, then people in the NFL will want to buy you like beef on the hoof."

Silence like death in the auditorium. Many people were stunned by this unusual valedictorian address.

"So, my fellow students, these remarks are not made in bitterness, only in the hope that we will each examine ourselves as we graduate from this institution. Examine our hopes, dreams, goals and motives. As for myself, my dream is still forming, not set in concrete, not yet crystal clear. But I feel deep down inside that I have a greater destiny than putting a ball through a hoop. Like I have said: I love the game. It has its place in our society. But it is not for me. I feel and I hope, that somehow, I will have something more, something deeper and meaningful, to contribute to our society.

"It is my hope that I may find and accomplish that something, and that each of you may discover how you are different, what is unique about you, and what you might contribute because of that uniqueness and differentness.

"Thank you."

CHAPTER 31

As summer moved on, Koro King's valedictorian address did not quickly fade out. It was the talk of the community. Many local newspapers printed it in its entirety. API and UPI and USA Today picked up the story and several national sports and TV news commentators read portions of the speech.

But Koro put it behind him and went to cowboying and ranch duties with the other ranch hands, at the King Cattle Ranch. Soon autumn moved into the Skeen Valley, or rather Indian summer. Warm days lingered on, but slowly the nights grew cool. A chill in the air or whatever scientific thing happens with leaves began to work its magic, turning the mountains along the Wasatch Front into flaming red, orange and yellow. Koro knew it was the hand of the Heavenly Father passing over the land, assuring all life that He was still in control.

Supper in the evening had been Gordo's Mexican specialty: beef enchiladas topped with cheese and guacamole, refried beans and Spanish rice mixed with diced green and red peppers. Koro provided a musical dessert afterward on the grand piano in the living room.

"That was a marvelous selection you played, my son," said Alfred, as Koro helped the old man out onto the porch to enjoy the setting sun. "Was it one of your own compositions?"

"Yes, Alf. It was taken from the music that comes to me from time to time. Mrs. Leckner has encouraged me to put my music on paper. She is having a friend on the west coast, a music publisher, copyright it for me and put it out as sheet music."

"Wonderful. Wonderful. I am happy to hear that."

They sat on the swinging couch at the south end of the long porch.

"I am so very proud of you, Koro," said the old man, after they had sat quietly for sometime, enjoying the setting sun in the lake far to the west. They also took in the sounds of evening and the smells of the season: mown hay, shocked grain, mellons and squash lying in the fields, and ripe apple smells. It was one of those rare evenings when the moon could be seen rising in the eastern sky, the sun setting in the west and the evening star in between. The world was especially quiet, as though holding its breath, waiting for some great event.

"Finding you in far away Africa and bringing you here gave my life new meaning," said old King. I knew you were an exceptional child, someone special, even when I first met you. I realized from the beginning that you could see beyond what others see and could hear what others couldn't. You would have liked one of our great ladies I had the privilege of meeting. Helen Keller. She could not see with her mortal eyes nor hear with her mortal ears. She had difficulty communicating. But she had a mind and imagination far beyond most of us.

"It has kept my mind young watching you grow, not just in body, but seeing you learn, blossom out, achieve, seeing your mental and spiritual growth." He turned and had to look up to his grandson. "Have you made any decisions as to 'What now?' Where is your life to go from here? You are welcome just to stay on at the ranch. It is yours, you know, if you so wish to remain."

"I have given much thought to many things, Alf. I have fulfilled my boyhood dream of being an American cowboy..."

"And you have become one of the best," cut in the old man.

"Thanks to your tutoring and my brother cowhands here at the ranch. But my dream is still out there somewhere, Alf. Out there in the world of people. I have thought that maybe I might be a teacher or a doctor or social worker. I have a strong need within me to heal people's wounds, to help them more with wounds of the mind and spirit rather than physical wounds perhaps.

"You have given me the world in a way, Alf. If you had not

brought me here, my choices would have been few. I would have become a warrior in our tribe. A warrior now protects his *kraal* and his people from danger. And he protects the cattle. That would have been my life until I became old. Then I would have become an elder in the tribe with the limited duties of the old Maasai men.

"But here... now... in this amazing land of America, there are unlimited choices. So many choices and decisions... choices and decisions... endless opportunities..." His voice trailed off.

"Yes. That is true," replied Alfred King quietly. "Do you mind if we go inside and continue our discussion? The night air gets a bit chilly in an old man's bones."

Koro helped him up and inside. They sat on the couch in front of the big living room window. Alfred often sat there and read or scribbled notes on a note pad he kept near the lamp on the end table by the couch. Koro went into the kitchen and brought out a dish of oatmeal cookies and a glass of milk for each of them.

"Do you know my most exciting and memorable moment since I came here, Alf?" asked Koro.

"When you rode the bronco at the rodeo? Or when you won the state basketball championship? Or when you were named class valedictorian?"

"Nope. Wrong on all guesses. The time I hold closest to my heart was when I first arrived here as a wide-eyed little boy and you hiked with me overnight into those beautiful mountains."

Old King wiped a tear from his eye. "I liked that too," he said.

They ate cookies and sipped at their milk. The sun had dropped into the lake. The horizon turned from pink to dark red to black. Koro turned on the lamp on the end table.

"We have visited almost every church from here to Salt Lake City, haven't we Alf?" he asked, changing the subject.

"I believe that we have."

"The feeling I get in most churches is good. Peaceful. I like the music, the singing, the study of scriptures and sermons. But one thing has always bothered me, Alf."

"What is that, my boy?"

"First, it is the feeling that there are so many different churches. And each one claims to be the true church, or to have the truth. They eventually want you to join or belong to their congregation. This makes them exclusive. Others who don't belong or join become outsiders. It pits us against them. They each establish different doctrines, dogma or rules that you must believe and follow.

"I would like a church to be more open. Open for worship, meditation, contemplation, prayer and discussion of ideas. My dream, Alf, is to be a minister of such a church. Perhaps my dream is unrealistic and that is why I haven't mentioned it before. Perhaps I am looking for a Utopian church. I see my own continent of Africa, almost every country there, torn with strife, wars, poverty, hunger, pain. I see much of the world in some kind of turmoil or chaos. People are searching for something. Even in this great country there is unrest, anxiety, people feeling alone, forgotten. I would really like to be able to sooth the pain of a small portion of my fellow beings."

"I have seen this dream in you for some time, my boy. Somehow I have known of your dream. It is a marvelous dream, Koro. Keep pursuing it and perhaps the way will open. But I won't be here to share your dream. My time is here to move on. I am ready to go on that next great adventure."

Koro looked at the old man. He could see the wrinkles of character in his tired face and the far away look in his eyes. He did not argue with his dear Alfred King. His African heritage made him accept as fact when someone said their mortal time was ending. He put his arm around his father's shoulders and gave him a squeeze. "I will miss you more than words can explain, Alf," he said softly.

"None of us can name the exact time or place," continued the old man. "But if I could arrange it, this is how I would like to die..." He moistened his lips and a smile turned up his lips and sparkled in his eyes. "It would be spring, probably May. I would be sitting in the shade of a huge weeping willow tree where a soft breeze was distributing the heavenly smell of lilacs from the yard. The laughter of children would be blowing dandelion parachutes to be shared with the breeze. From an open window in the house would drift the musical notes of Claire de Luen dispersed from a well played harp. A few popcorn clouds would be sailing across an otherwise pale robin-egg-colored sky."

He coughed and wiped at his eyes, and continued in a hoarse voice. "Clouds have always made a more interesting sky, I think. I would be eating a banana split, smiling and savoring each mouthful until my hand could no longer lift the heavy spoon to my lips... and I would be gone."

An owl hooted and crickets sang their chorus through the open door.

"I have traveled the world over, Koro. But I have never found a place I love more than right here in these valleys of the mountains. And when I am dying I hope my last words will be, 'Oh what a marvelous journey—the one just past and the one ahead.'

"You better get to bed now, my boy. I have enjoyed this time we have spent together. Just now. And all of our past years. Would you put that blanket on me, please, and turn out the lamp. I think I will just lay my head back for awhile and enjoy the night sounds."

"I have enjoyed the years also, Alf. I have enjoyed them immensely," the boy said, as he spread the blanket on the old man's lap and left him alone.

CHAPTER 32

Koro's music awakened him before dawn just as the first streaks of gray distinguished the mountains from the sky. It was still dark inside the house. No one had stirred as yet, not even Gordo, who always arose earlier than anyone else to start breakfast cooking. His music was playing a rousing, jubilant tune that could best be described as a spiritual or a religious march, like *Onward Christian Soldiers*. The music was powerful as any he had ever heard. It pulled him like a magnet, out of bed, down the hall to the living room.

He could make out Alf's form still asleep on the couch where he had left him. He did not want to disturb him, so turned to go back to bed. But the music would not let him. It pulled him back beside the old man. He turned on the lamp on the end table beside the couch and wondered why his music arose in such a crescendo. He shook the old man's shoulder gently and his head fell down to his chest.

The realization suddenly came to him that the old man had slept right into the next adventure. He had gone beyond the veil. Alfred King was dead.

Koro noticed then the open note pad lying by the lamp. Alf had written something on it. He picked it up and read: *Oh what a marvelous journey—the one just past and the one ahead.*

Koro's vision blurred as he placed the note pad back on the table.

...

The funeral was held in the Mormon Stake Center because it would accommodate the largest crowd in Skeen. Alfred King was known as a cattleman far and wide. He was also known for his photography and writing. But mostly he was known for his kindness and generosity.

Besides people from all parts of Utah, they came from Jerome, Burley, Preston and Pocatello, and other towns in Idaho. They came from the Four Corners area where he had done much cattle buying and selling: Durango, Cortez, Mancos and Grand Junctions, Colorado. Farmington, Shiprock, Santa Fe and Albuquerque in New Mexico. Kayenta and over to Phoenix in Arizona. And Evanston, Rock Springs, Star Valley and Cheyenne, Wyoming. Yes, Alfred King was a well known and well liked man.

Many paid tribute in words and music. Koro paid his respects by playing his own composition on the organ. Many tears were shed. But those who knew him best knew that he was ready and expectant to move on to this new and exciting adventure in the unknown. He was ready. He had told Koro that his time had arrived.

Alfred King was buried in the little cemetery on the hillside overlooking Skeen and the lake beyond, in the place he loved beyond all others.

PART IV

THE CHURCH OF MANY COLORS

CHAPTER 33

Two days after Alfred King's funeral, Richard took a phone call from Ed Withers, long time friend, attorney and executor of King's estate.

"Richard, this is Ed Withers, Alfred King's attorney. Alf made me executor of his will. He always came to my office, but now I need to come out there to the ranch. I've heard so much about your fellows, that I feel I know you. Alf always spoke of you as his family. I need to go over the will. Could you get the bunch of you together? Would it be all right if I spent a few days out there?"

"You bet, Mr. Withers. Come on out and stay as long as you like. We would love to have you. Maybe we could even make a cowboy out of you. And of course we need to know the contents of Mr. King's will, so the ranch can keep on operating."

"Thank you, Richard. How about getting there next Monday?"

"Okay by me, Mr. Withers. We'll look forward to your arrival."

"Thanks again, Richard. I need to get away from the city for awhile. And maybe I'll take you up on that cowboying."

...

Ed Withers arrived on Monday at the King Cattle Ranch in time for lunch. Richard introduced him around. When he met Koro he lookd up in shock and surprise. "Holy cow, Koro! When Alf asked me to do the adoption papers on a little boy from Africa, I guess... well, I suppose in my mind I still had you as a little boy.

Time sort of gets away from me. I see now that you can't be called little in any sense of the word."

They all laughed and seated Ed at the table for lunch. He immediately felt accepted as family by these rugged cowboys. Ed Withers forgot about business, city, traffic and noise for the next few days, as these happy ranch hands set about teaching this eager city dude to learn some cowboying.

"You ever been on a horse, Mr. Withers?" asked Larry in his quiet, serious manner.

"The answer is 'No.' And I must admit that horses rather terrify me. But I am anxious to give it a go."

"Great," said Dex, leading out a big sorrel mare. "This here horse is as kind and gentle as any critter has a right to be. Her name is Clementine."

"Here, I'll help you mount up for your first time," said Chuck, cupping his hands. "Put your left foot in my hands. That's it. Now throw your right leg up and over the saddle while I give you a boost."

Ed looked pleased as a jockey who had just won the Kentucky Derby, as he adjusted himself in the saddle. "Now what?" he asked.

"You just kind of cluck your tongue," said Richard, making the proper tongue sounds. "Then you flick the reins lightly and she'll go for you."

"This one neck reins, so pull the reins left to turn left and right to turn right. Easy as steering a car," added Dex. "We'll soon have you as bow-legged as any cowhand that rode the range."

The next few days, Ed Withers was in horse heaven. He proved to be a good learner, although at night he was so sore and stiff that he had to be helped out of the saddle.

"The cure, Ed, is a hot bath and rubdown with this," said Koro, handing him a bottle of liniment and rubbing alcohol. "And of course, the magic therapy of Gordo's fine supper that will be waiting for you."

...

Finally Ed Withers got to the matter of business and gathered them all together in the living room for the matter of the will. They sprawled leisurely on the couch and the soft upholstered chairs around the room.

"First I wish to say how much I have enjoyed my short stay here with you," he began. "Alf was right. You guys are the greatest bunch in the world. I can see why he considered you as his family.

"Second, I'd like to say, to prepare you, that I don't think any of you realize how wealthy Alfred King was. As you know, he was low-key about money matters. Besides this ranch, his kingdom and favorite place, he owned real estate all over the world. He owned hotels, office buildings, two banks, a chain of restaurants, athletic clubs, on and on. I dare say that Alfred King was most likely one of the wealthiest men in America, though few people knew of it."

Surprise shone in their faces. They had always thought that they were working for just another wealthy cattleman.

"Alf was also one of the most generous and compassionate human being I have ever known," continued Ed Withers. "He helped many people in his quiet way throughout his life. In his will he left large sums to many charitable causes. Among his favorite charities were the Primary Children's Medical Center, the Salvation Army, the Shriner's Hospital, Interplast, the Mormon Church and several other churches.

"I am not going to read the will formally; it is too long and a lot of it won't concern you here. I will just cover the parts that refer to you people. I will give you each a copy of your own that you may read at your leisure."

He opened his attache case and took out several thick, brown envelopes and handed one to each of them.

"Okay. Now the parts concerning each of you. He leaves this beautiful ranch house and everything in it to Koro, Gordo, and Richard. He commends Gordo and his son, Richard, for being with him these many years and serving so loyally. The rest of the entire ranch: buildings, land and cattle, he leaves to all of you divided into equal shares."

A cheer went up from their happy faces.

"In addition, he leaves Gordo and Richard five million dollars each to use as they see fit..."

"Wow!" yelled Dex. "Rich, now you are really rich."

Richard Gonzalez smiled while tears streamed down his cheeks. Gordo wiped at his eyes also.

"Oh yes, you all should know that he made sure that Mrs. Leckner would be taken care of for the rest of her life. And grab onto your seats again. To Larry, Chuck and Dex he leaves one million dollars each."

Another cheer.

"Can you believe it?" said Chuck. "Us dirty, no-good cowboys are millionaires."

"Now, hold onto your hats," continued Ed Withers. "I will read this part of the will as he had it dictated: "To my son, Koro, who brought joy and new life to me in my old years, I leave the sum of *one hundred million dollars* because he will know how to put it to good use."

Stunned silence.

More silence.

Finally Koro said quietly, almost in a whisper, "Yes, I do know how I will put it to good use, and Alf must have known even before I did." Then louder he said, "Ed, could you stay on a couple of more days? I would like to hire you as my attorney. I have a lot of work in mind for you to do. Would you accept me as a client?"

"You bet I will, Koro. And I'll be happy to stay longer. I like it here."

"Then, let's all meet here again tomorrow after our chores are done. I have some things to say that you all should hear." To Richard he said, "Could I see you for a few minutes, Rich?"

"Sure."

The others all left. Koro and Richard sat again on the couch.

"I've been thinking, pondering really, for a long time what I want to do with my life," Koro began, seriously. "I've talked a lot with Alf. He must have anticipated my decision. That's why he left me that tremendous amount of money." He looked into his friend and brother's eyes. "I am leaving the ranch, Rich."

"It's no surprise to me, Koro, but go on."

"I want to use the money to build a church, a different kind of church... in a slum area. A church for all people, all colors, all races, mostly poor and needy. Those who are hungering for spiritual food. I want to be the minister of such a church and preach hope to them. I want to spred the message of love and peace... the message spread by the one known as the Prince of Peace... Jesus of Nazareth."

"I want to go with you," said Richard Gonzalez suddenly, following the quiet after Koro's announcement. "I think I have always known of your secret dream; at least I have felt that I knew of it. Take me with you, Koro, wherever it is that your music leads you. Ever since that night when you told me of your music and how it came about, I have wanted to follow where it led you."

"Are you sure? Do you know what you are leaving? Your life is ranching, always has been. You are foreman here."

"My life is ready for a change. I will appoint Larry as foreman. He is finally ready to marry that sweetheart that he has courted forever. She is a widow with three kids. They will need this place to live in. Larry will love it and make an excellent foreman."

Koro smiled. "Yes, you can come. I will need your help. Let's do it. We will tell them tomorrow."

CHAPTER 34

They were gathered together again. Koro stood to make his announcement. "What I have to say may be a surprise to some of you." He turned to Attorney Ed Withers. "Ed, by agreeing to take me on as a client you will have your work cut out for you. Here is my plan, my dream if you will. I want you to buy me fifty acres in the middle of a large city ghetto: Chicago, New York, Detroit, or preferably out on the west coast in the Los Angeles area, for what I have in mind. I like the warmer climate also."

Everyone sat spellbound, caught totally by surprise.

"On that fifty acres I want to build a unique church, which I shall help design. And I would like to be the minister of that church. Ed, is this an impossibility? A dream of such magnitude, of such a Utopia? Is it possible to acquire fifty acres, build a church, and arrange for me a minister's license, although I have never been to a divinity school or a theological seminary?"

Ed Withers was grinning jubilantly. "Impossible or not, I like those kind of challenges, Koro. Let's go at it and see what we can do. I will leave first thing in the morning and give it my full throttle."

"Good. I appreciate that, Ed. And will you set up a perpetuating fund for such a venture. Use what you need of my funds also to accomplish our goals. Richard now has something to say."

"Another surprise," said Richard Gonzalez, smiling. "I am going with Koro to be a side-kick in his dream project. We are both relinquishing our shares of the ranch house to be divided between my father, Gordo, and Larry." He turned to Larry, whose face was frozen in shock. "You are finally going to marry that lovely lady of yours, aren't you, Larry?"

Larry's face went red as the reddest rose. He stammered in his usual bashful way, "Well... er... well... yeah. We're planning to get married."

"Okay, then I appoint you as the new foreman of the King Cattle Company. You can bring your little lady and her kids here to live, and Gordo can still cook for you all so she won't have to work so hard. And your second order of business will be to get some more ranch hands to keep things going here, even if Chuck and Dex decide to stay on."

They both nodded and Chuck said, "This is our life. This is where we belong."

"All right," said Ed Withers. "Let's get with it. We all have our work cut out for us. Koro, I'll be in touch. Don't know when or where, but I'll be in touch.

...

And they all did have plenty of work to keep them busy, winding up affairs at the ranch. Larry got married to his woman in a small ceremony with a few of her family and his ranch partners in attendance. He moved, with her and the kids into the ranch house, and Koro moved out to the bunkhouse. Five new cowhands were hired.

Six weeks passed and no word from Ed Withers. Koro began to have doubts about his plan. Maybe his dream was the impossible dream. Then on the seventh week a telegram came from Withers:

Property acquired. Come to Los Angeles.

CHAPTER 35

Koro and Richard left with tearful goodbyes.

Richard Gonzalez found a Mexican family, near the site in Los Angeles, to board with. He was delighted to learn that they had known his parents in their little village in Chiapas, Mexico. He was even more delighted to meet their daughter, a dark-eyed beauty with whom he immediately fell in love.

Koro lived in a little construction shack on the property. Ed Withers had been able, through much wheeling and dealing, to acquire the property in the middle of a ghetto in Los Angeles. They had to relocate a few families, but most of the buildings were vacant, crumbling structures that had been condemned.

Wrecking crews demolished all structures. Earth movers and trucks hauled debris away. Caterpillars leveled the land. The work of construction began.

The huge black man, sweat glistening on his body, and the little wiry Mexican with the big cowboy hat and boots, became familiar figures on the site. They were the first to be there and the last to quit each day. They carried hod for the rock and brick layers. They placed rebar, poured cement, helped dig footings. They were used to long days on the ranch. No one could out-work them. They gained the respect of all the construction workers.

Koro admired the skill of the construction workers. He complimented them daily and called them craftsmen and artisans. He liked hose who worked hard and created with their hands works of beauty: the hewers of stone, the layers of brick, the formers of cement, the sawers of woods and drivers of nails, the cutters and fitters of glass. The connectors of electricity, and fitters of pipes and plumbing. The brushers and spreaders of paint. Craftsmen.

Artisans. All skilled, each expert in their specialty. He loved these hard workers and worked shoulder to shoulder with them. They in turn, loved him and the little Mexican.

Each day, Koro, Richard and Ed Withers met with the architects, the master artists of building, to make sure that every stone was laid to perfection, every nail driven precisely.

Gradually the structure arose from the earth, higher and higher, stone upon stone. Soon the landscapers, artists with nature's products, came and began the outside beautification.

Near the completion of the project, Ed Withers arrived with a wide smile on his tired face. He called a work recess and summoned all workers in a circle.

"I want all of you who have worked on this magnificent project to know that this big fellow who has been working with you every day, is the new minister of this beautiful edifice that you all have built."

He handed Koro a fine leather folder. "Open it up, my boy," he said. "Inside is your official minister's license. You are the youngest licensed minister in the country. You are now authorized to marry folks, bury them, preach to them, and provide them with any and all of their spiritual needs."

All of the workers cheered and clapped wildly while tears rolled unashamedly down the big black man's face.

"Thank you. Thank you all. Since you have all done such a fine job and the project is near completion, I invite all of you to stay after work today to the biggest, tastiest steak fry with all of the trimmings, that you have ever eaten. And I will personally, with the help of Richard and Ed, charcoal the steaks to your individual specifications."

More wild cheering, as each worker stepped forward to shake Koro, Richard, and Ed's hands.

CHAPTER 36

It was finished.

Completed.

A creation of beauty and splendor.

The Church of Many Colors was its name.

It stood in the midst of squalor and decay. A haven, an oasis, a long sentinel of what-could-be. An impossible dream made possible. Its five spires reached toward heaven. On the middle and tallest spire, a golden angel perched, as though descending from vapors of heaven. Its stones hauled from mountains far away, built to withstand the prevailing pollutions and perhaps the trembling of the earth, and floods and fires.

Massive solid oak doors opened to the entrance, with intricate carvings upon them. Above the doors, an enormous oval stained glass window depicted the world, its nations in many colors. Leaded, stained windows lined each side of the building, with a native of a different country on each one.

The interior walls were lined in walnut and teak wood. The pews were of oak and birch. The podium of many different inlaid woods. Behind the podium were the golden pipes of a pipe organ reaching to the ceiling, imported from Switzerland.

On the outside, narrow, winding stone paths wove their way through grounds of tender grass, shrubs and flowers of many colors. Three ponds of various sizes and shapes were placed strategically on the grounds. One was in a grove of elm and maple trees and was deep and still, filled with large gold fish from Japan. Another featured a waterfall of recycled water, turning a quaint wooden water wheel under a weeping birch tree. The third was an oval, shallow pond with water lilies, fish of many colors and frogs. It was surrounded by various types of palm trees.

Benches were placed near these ponds and other places throughout the grounds where people could sit to enjoy nature, contemplate and pray. It was spring. Birds came. Butterflies and bees came. Chipmunks and squirrels were imported, small creatures hardly ever seen by people of these slums and ghettos.

Flyers were distributed. Posters were pinned throughout surrounding communities, announcing that all were welcome. Please come. At first, a few came hesitantly, shyly. Then more came. Finally, they came in droves.

Grand Opening.

Easter Sunday.

The church was filled to its fifteen hundred capacity and overflowed outside to the grounds. The doors and windows of the chapel were left open.

The audience sat in anticipation as a tall, elegant black man wearing a magnificent deep red robe, approached the podium. His head was shaved. From each ear hung a gold circle. His feet were encased in plain sandals. He spoke with a booming resonant voice.

"Welcome. Welcome to the *Church of Many Colors*. My name is Koro King. I am from Kenya in East Africa. This gentleman sitting to my right on the stand, wearing faded jeans and cowboy boots, is my brother and partner, Richard Gonzalez. He comes from the country of Mexico. We are dressed in attire that we feel comfortable in. And also to let you know that no one will be kept out of this chapel because they don't have a suit or tie or Sunday dress. Please wear what you have and what you feel comfortable in.

"Also there will be no money collected in this church. If you have money to spare, use it to help your neighbors who have less or none. We have established a perpetuating fund and have hired permanent custodians, ground keepers and others needed to maintain this beautiful edifice.

"If you wish to contribute your time, we welcome you to vol-

unteer on one of the committees we will establish. We want to
provide activities for youth, outreach programs for the old, the
disabled and the handiapped. Committees to visit the sick and
those in hospitals, those that have mental and alcohol or drug
problems, those that grieve or mourn the loss of loved ones, those
that are trying to raise children alone. So you see we illicit all of
your help in providing these services to your neighbors and fellow
beings.

"This church has been named *The Church of Many Colors* for a
reason. No one will be turned away or made to feel unwelcome
because of race, religious beliefs, social status or color of skin. We
welcome Browns, Tans, Blacks, Whites, Reds, Yellows or even
Green, if there are such. This is to be an every-day chapel. It will
always be open for your meditation and prayers.

"We hope to invite ministers of many religions to preach from
this pulpit. But there will be no sectarian dogma or doctrine
preached unless it embodies the two principles of Peace and Love.
And peace and love are eternally inter-connected. One cannot abide
without the other. YOU do not have to belong to anything; you
do not have to join, to enter this church. If you do not know one
another's names please use the terms of Sister or Brother. We are
all children of the one great God, although we may know Him by
many different names.

"I will now tell you my secret that has brought me here. This
magnificent building was built by the money of one of the most
loving, compassionate, kind human beings that I have had the
privilege of knowing: the only father I have known, who was also
grandfather, brother and friend to me. Alfred King was his name.
He has now gone on that next journey into the unknown, but his
spirit will be felt always in this chapel.

"But my secret, my Brothers and Sisters is that all of my life I
have been guided by a marvelous, mystical music that enters into
my mind from somewhere that I have only vague memories of. It
has always been pulling me, leading me somewhere. That somewhere, I now know, is here. This..." He spread his arms in a sweep-

ing gesture. "This building and mostly you people are the fulfill-
ment of my dream, my music.

"A talented, dear lady taught me to write my music onto paper and to play it for others. Now, during this first public service
in this church, I will play for you my music on this powerful
organ, a finely crafted instrument imported from the country of
Switzerland.

"Sit back, close your eyes and ponder, each one of you upon
your own music, while I play for you my music, which, I hope,
speaks of Love and Peace."

He walked to the organ, sat upon the organ bench, closed his
eyes and placed his huge hands upon the keys. Music came from
the golden pipes like a music never heard before. The people wept.
Some of them knelt in the isles in the attitude of prayer. The music drifted out of the open doors and windows. It was caught by
the breeze and carried to surrounding communities.

The-Boy-Who-Hears-Music played his music as never before.
He was inspired. The people fell under its spell as though in a
trance. They could feel its spirit of Love and Peace, as the wind
carried its melody and message farther and farther.

And perhaps... just perhaps... some day, it might be carried to
all the far corners of the earth.

THE END